Left-Handed Dreams

Left-Handed Dreams

FRANCESCA DURANTI

DELPHINIUM BOOKS

HARRISON, NEW YORK   ENCINO, CALIFORNIA

LIBRARY OF CONGRESS CATALOGING-IN-PUBLICATION DATA

DURANTI, FRANCESCA

[SOGNI MANCINI. ENGLISH]

LEFT-HANDED DREAMS/ BY FRANCESCA DURANTI.-1ST ED.

P. CM.

ISBN 1-883285-19-4

PQ4864.U68 S6413 2000

853'.914-DC21   00-022737

FIRST EDITION

10 9 8 7 6 5 4 3 2 1

DISTRIBUTED BY HARPERCOLLINS PUBLISHERS

PRINTED IN THE UNITED STATES OF AMERICA ON ACID-FREE PAPER

DESIGNED BY KRYSTYNA SKALSKI

ACKNOWLEDGMENTS

I would like to thank Arthur Coppotelli with great affection. Without him I never would have been able to translate this book into English.

BGT 12.38 01/01

Left-Handed Dreams

Saturday: Risotto alla Milanese

I

They say she died at seven-thirty in the morning, just as my plane was landing at Leonardo da Vinci. The pilot had circled over Rome for almost an hour trying to find his way in the autumn storm that was raging over the city. Eventually he made his way through the clouds and let the plane drop like a stone in a well. When the wheels touched the runway I let go of the armrests and looked at my watch: seven-thirty, exactly.

I could put together a lecture for you students from all this, beginning just at that point, because more than once, in the days that followed, I thought about my arriving the moment she was departing, puzzled by some mesmerizing although indecipherable implication of destiny's perfect timing.

Let's begin there, from my landing at Leonardo da Vinci, after my sister Carmelina's urgent call.

Racing along the endless people-movers in the airport

terminal, I barely made it to the connecting DC-8 that took me on a bumpy climb back over the storm clouds. Thirty-five minutes to fly to Pisa, another thirty-five for a taxi to take me to Nugola Vecchia, where my mother was already laid out in her black dress, her hands folded over her missal, her face shiny smooth, her nostrils transparent like one of the wax saints in the churches of our native Lucania.

Carmelina stood by the coffin, she too dressed in black, flanked by her husband and her two sisters-in-law. The four of them were stiff and solemn, like carabinieri standing guard at the tomb of the Unknown Soldier. She stepped forward and embraced me, her chest heaving with sighs of disapproval.

"She asked about you right till the last . . . she hoped to see you just once more," she said.

"I hoped the same," I replied.

My sister Carmelina—Milly now—speaks with a strained Tuscan accent that in nature doesn't exist. She aspirates her Cs so hard that she's had to be operated on twice for polyps on her vocal chords. Out of respect for our Lucania, I make an effort when I'm talking to her to bring back an echo of our native accent, as unnatural as hers by now.

My sister was born when our family had already moved to Nugola. She married a dentist and now lives in Livorno. She's lost touch with the past. She doesn't know anything about Lucania, because she hasn't been back to the South except for a few Christmases many years ago. Though I'm older, I can't remember those visits very clearly either. But it's as if she had never even breathed that special air that my parents had brought with them from Lucania and that permeated our house. It wasn't just the southern accent that they both retained until they died, it was more the Christmas and Easter customs, the food, certain kitchen utensils, the way bread and preserves were made.

What never came up were facts about the past. One in particular I would need a few hours after my mother's death, one only she could provide. That's why I find that whim of fate so puzzlingly meaningful: why let me get there just as she departed, she who had probably been the start of it all?

2

The coffin had been set up in the dining room. There was a humble smell of cleanliness—furniture polish, laundry soap, floor wax. The shutters were closed in mourning, but the sounds of traffic from the highway in the valley below could be heard through the open windows. People came, mostly Carmelina's friends, who embraced us, stood a moment before the coffin, and then left. "She looks as if she were sleeping," they all said. It wasn't true, fortunately. Mamma's face had the beauty and incomparable dignity of death, as was proper. I once went to a funeral parlor in New York to pay my respects to an old colleague's dead wife. I remember that when I saw her so tarted-up I couldn't help thinking that poor Mrs. Garrison looked as if she were about to step out of her coffin and go hit the streets. Looking at my beautiful mamma, I thanked heaven that my country hadn't yet adopted the American practice of putting makeup on the dead.

The wreaths began to arrive and soon converted the clean smell of the house into something stagnant and sickly sweet. I let myself be embraced by many callers I didn't know until I couldn't stand it.

"I'm going out to stretch my legs," I finally said to Carmelina. Then I added, "I've been in a plane all night," but she shrugged her shoulders without a word to forgive my desertion.

I hadn't been to Nugola Vecchia in years. Usually my mother came to see me in America. Whenever I went over to spend Christmas in Tuscany, we would all go to my sister's in Livorno. And the few times I went to Italy on summer holidays we would rent a house together a few kilometers south, along the rocky coast of Castiglioncello. Although Nugola, where I was raised and where my sister was born, is only a half-hour drive from either Livorno or Castiglioncello, I hadn't made the trip back in a very long time.

It was unrecognizable, defaced by an ugly bunch of houses that had been built on the hill called Poggio di Mezzo, the Treasure Island of my childhood. Back then it had been only a huge sand dune covered with dense woods of oaks and hornbeam, and here and there a few pines, holm oaks, laurels and arbutus that kept their green leaves all winter. That's what I miss in Central Park, so bleak from Thanksgiving till spring.

Students, I'm talking about over thirty years ago. I know how you figure time at your age. Thirty years for you is like a tunnel dug into the past where one gets immediately lost in a darkness of immeasurable length. And I actually had the same feeling myself as I tried to remember the dune as it had been—a perfect dome covered with trees, with a chunk missing on the north side where they once used to excavate sand.

On that yellow, creamy slope, the bee-eaters had dug their nests and would come back every year in April, bringing with them the enchantment of their brilliant tropical coloring. Their churring could be heard from afar. One morning in spring I'd wake up and hear them coming back.

There was another small area, right on the hilltop, where trees and bushes didn't grow. Perfectly round, it was carpeted with blackish moss forming a magic circle—perhaps the site of a charcoal cone long ago—surrounded by a dense Mediterranean thicket. That was the Elephants' Ballroom.

Every day I would go to my Treasure Island. Beneath the tangle of heather, I would find mushrooms, which my mother would dry and sell, and wild asparagus. I would pick arbutus berries for my father to make illegal grappa, or look for other treasures, like sharp white-and black-ringed hedgehog quills, thirty to thirty-five centimeters long, or fossil shells millions of years old, going back to a time when Nugola was covered by the sea.

All this had now disappeared. I walked across the village from one end to the other, as far as the cemetery, and back again to what once had been Poggio di Mezzo. The dune had been leveled and squared off, the Elephants' Ballroom no longer recognizable. Which one of the parking lots occupied the area that used to be carpeted with blackish moss? I didn't have a point of reference because all the trees had been ripped out and replaced mostly by cement, or by straggly hedges of an obnoxious blue evergreen, or by even more incongruous forsythia bushes at the entrance of the desolate condos. There was an unbelievably ugly pizzeria where the sand pit used to be, and not a sign of the bee-eaters.

I stayed on in Nugola for two days, putting my mother's things away or wandering aimlessly about the countryside. The village had become a squalid suburb. The farmers from Lucania, who came north soon after us, had now left or died. Others from the South and those few genuine Tuscans who hadn't been citified before our arrival were all changed, like my hill, Poggio di Mezzo. When Carmelina came over to help me pack our mother's things, or when we spoke on the phone, I tried to remind her of the Elephants' Ballroom, the mushrooms, the bee-eaters. But I understood perfectly that she only pretended to remember, not to disappoint me by admitting that her memory and mine had selected our recollections in opposite ways, erasing what we had in common and turning us into strangers. I've already mentioned her forced, overdone Tuscan accent that de-southerned her. But then, with the death of our mother, even the memory of Nugola, where we had been poor farmers, had become a cumbersome link to a past she no longer needed. I realized that from then on, family to her meant the tribe of her husband's

3

They were both at the cemetery, Mr. Ceccarelli and Dr. Paoletti, but with so many people there, I didn't have the time to talk to them as I would have liked.

So the next day, driving my mother's old Fiat, I went to Stagno to visit Mr. Ceccarelli, who had given me work in the cafeteria from the day my father died until I went back to school. He was older and more deaf.

"How's America?" he asked.

"So-so," I answered. Every time I go to see him, he asks the same question and I give him the same answer. He emerged from his kitchen, drying his hands on a white tea towel, and we went to sit at a table in the empty cafeteria.

"Is your work going well?" I asked.

"I'm satisfied," he said. "I have two Filipino girls now who do what you and your mother did. They're slow but very thorough. And you? When will you be returning to Italy?"

"To do what?"

"What you do there. Don't we have universities in th country? Haven't you been away from home long enough Even this was part of the script, like the last thing he said I was leaving: "Have you been to see Dr. Paoletti?"

"I'm on my way there now."

every so often; they bring me small meals to put in the freezer. But not one of them is as intelligent as you were." That too is something he repeats every time. He had shrunk to a mere shadow. His voice too had changed.

"Maybe it's because I'm old and don't really desire anything anymore, but I think I'll never be keen on helping young people—male or female—get on with their studies. These days too many of them go to college anyway. The dumbest jackasses get a degree and then don't know what to do with it." That's what he told me and I'm afraid he was right. Then he added, "But you were something else. It was worth it, and you've proved that."

Before leaving, I dashed down to buy the ingredients I needed to prepare him a perfect *risotto alla milanese*—with beef marrow, onion, saffron, butter, parsley and lemon zest—cooked to just the right creaminess. I set the little table he always uses now, since he eats alone; but I moved it to the window, facing toward the sunset on the sea. The day was clear and the island of Gorgona was visible on the horizon. I used his splendid silver, his family crystal and china. I arranged the yellow roses I had bought in a Limoges vase. I sat him at the table and kissed him good-bye.

"You'll see, you'll enjoy this," I said, but I didn't believe it myself. I walked along the canal, thinking that maybe the next time I came to Italy Dr. Paoletti wouldn't be around anymore.

*   *   *

I stayed on for two days in those desolate rooms that had been my mother's home. It wasn't the farm house I had been brought up in; this was smaller, modern and dull. She had moved her things and herself there without much enthusiasm. The preserves she had continued to put up every summer were loaded into the Fiat and taken directly up to the eleventh floor of an anonymous high-rise apartment building in the city where my sister lived. There they stood, incongruously lined up on the shelves of her Scavolini kitchen in purple Formica: the sun-dried tomatoes, the bottle of olive oil with garlic cloves and hot peppers, the aubergine marinade, the pickled red onions.

In Mamma's house everything was clean and in perfect order, and yet those four rooms seemed never to have been lived in. I thought that perhaps my mother hadn't lived anywhere for years, from the time I had left for America and my sister had married. From that time her heart was not with her anymore, but half with me and half with Carmelina and her children.

I didn't even unpack the small bag I had brought with me. It was there sitting on a chair, as if I were staying in a hotel. From the window I couldn't see the country I remembered, but only the dismal suburbs that were gradually cementing together the beautiful old Tuscan cities and villages. I missed my New York apartment. I even missed all of you. I missed the Machine that was waiting for me on its cart next to my bed.

There was nothing left for me to do in Nugola. I had arrived too late to hold my mother's hand while she was dying. It was too late for everything. I called Alitalia to change to an earlier flight to New York.

Some play solitaire; for years I've played bridge by myself, every morning before going to work. I deal out the cards and play all the four players' hands, forcing each one not to remember his partner's or the opponents' cards.

The evening of the funeral, as I wandered unhappily from one room to another, I remembered I hadn't brought cards for my solitary morning bridge game. So before going to bed I went out to buy a deck at the local *caffé*.

That too had changed for the worse: plastic everywhere; new, indifferent owners; no one playing *tresette* at the tables. Only one thing was the same as in the old days: the cards they sold were not the bridge cards I always use, but the narrow ones they use to play *tresette*, made of cheap coated paper with grey backs. The numbers were not marked at the four corners, but just at the upper left and lower right.

I paid for the cards, walked around for a bit, and went home. I made myself a cheese omelette and went to bed early. From the open window I could hear the bitchy voice of a TV talk-show hostess.

She was saying, "What counts is keeping up your capacity for indignation."

She didn't need to be concerned. All her guests were indignant at each other and argued in very loud voices until the end of the show. Then a western came on and I finally fell asleep, lulled by the peaceful crackling of the Winchester 73s.

The morning after, I got up to make myself coffee and took it back to bed. When I opened North's hand to begin my morning bridge game, I couldn't see the numbers, because each upper left corner, except the last, was hidden by the overlapping card. That was strange, unless it was a faulty deck that had been printed in reverse. I thought about this later, while I was on the phone with Mr. Ceccarelli. I remembered that he kept the same kind of cards under the cash register at the cafeteria for the workers who played tresette during lunch break. I asked him to check out a deck.

"Upper left and lower right," he said. "There's nothing wrong with them. You're just holding them the wrong way."

That was when the question came to my mind, one that my mother more than anybody else could have answered. The telephone, same as in the old house, was in the kitchen: on the same sideboard, set at the same angle on the same neatly pressed doily, along with a picture of Pope John and the sewing basket. I recalled the day I brought home the first dress I had bought with my own money—pink linen with a square neckline. I was trying it on in front of the mirror in the bedroom I shared with Carmelina. She was sitting cross-legged on her bed, reading Mickey Mouse comics.

"It's too big in the waist," she declared. She was right.

I got the sewing basket and tried to alter the dress on my own without asking my mother for help. We used to split household chores among us. I helped Mother with the cooking and pickling, and I also took care of the garden and the chickens, did small carpenter jobs, and was the house electrician besides. But I had never done the laundry, the ironing, or the sewing. Even little Carmelina was better at all that than I was.

She had stopped reading and was looking at me with a critical eye. At a certain point she remarked, "You'll never get it right. It's taken you half an hour just to thread the needle because you're doing it backwards. And you are even sewing backwards."

So the thirty-year-old incident came back to me. A kind of symmetry of mind. I always try to instill in you a certain *esprit de géométrie*, as you know, and this is the right moment to apply it. The dicotyledonous theory—let's call it that—surfaces here and is immediately confirmed.

I said good-bye to Mr. Ceccarelli, hung up the phone, picked up the cards, and fanned them out so I could read the numbers. But it wasn't natural for me to hold them that way. So I tried holding the cards in my right hand and playing with my left; this way I could read the numbers, but it didn't work; it was as if my fingers were tied by invisible strings.

*   *   *

I called my sister to tell her I was leaving earlier. She didn't object.

"By the way," I ventured. It was useless, but I had to try.

"As far as you know, was I left-handed when I was small?"

"I can't say, really. I wasn't around when you were small. I have no idea."

"But would you say Mamma was the kind of person who would force me to use my right hand . . . to correct me if I were left-handed?"

That was a stupid question and Carmelina laughed.

"Would she? My dear, she was a peasant. She dressed in black. She went to mass every morning. She was the Rule personified. The quintessence of discipline and conformism. For her there was only one way to do things right, and any other way was wrong. You know that. You do the laundry on Mondays, you bake your bread on Fridays, you eat with your right, you write with your right, you cross yourself with your right, you cook eel for Christmas Eve and lamb for Easter. My Riccardo is left-handed, and I had a job trying to stop Mamma from tying his left hand into a bag so that he'd have to use his right."

"You mean Riccardo is left-handed?"

"Yes, and even the little one, I think. Right now, the only thing he knows how to do is suck his thumb, and he sucks his left one."

the area that used to be carpeted with blackish moss? I didn't have a point of reference because all the trees had been ripped out and replaced mostly by cement, or by straggly hedges of an obnoxious blue evergreen, or by even more incongruous forsythia bushes at the entrance of the desolate condos. There was an unbelievably ugly pizzeria where the sand pit used to be, and not a sign of the bee-eaters.

I stayed on in Nugola for two days, putting my mother's things away or wandering aimlessly about the countryside. The village had become a squalid suburb. The farmers from Lucania, who came north soon after us, had now left or died. Others from the South and those few genuine Tuscans who hadn't been citified before our arrival were all changed, like my hill, Poggio di Mezzo. When Carmelina came over to help me pack our mother's things, or when we spoke on the phone, I tried to remind her of the Elephants' Ballroom, the mushrooms, the bee-eaters. But I understood perfectly that she only pretended to remember, not to disappoint me by admitting that her memory and mine had selected our recollections in opposite ways, erasing what we had in common and turning us into strangers. I've already mentioned her forced, overdone Tuscan accent that de-southerned her. But then, with the death of our mother, even the memory of Nugola, where we had been poor farmers, had become a cumbersome link to a past she no longer needed. I realized that from then on, family to her meant the tribe of her husband's blondish sisters. So enthusiastically had she been mingling with them year after year that even her alien dark eyes and hair had blended in, become domesticated. That's how she is. Some people have to forget in order to move on—like some Italian-Americans who can't speak the language of their forebears, and who name their children Dexter, Savile, Sean, Kenneth.

My eyes will always be black and my hair will go grey but never yellow. I was a year old when we left Potenza—and yet I don't feel I'd be myself without the memories of Lucania that my mother passed on to me. Then there are the memories of Tuscany, the Tuscan colors of Treasure Island, the cafeteria at the Stanic refinery, the sea cliffs of Calafuria, the University of Pisa, and lastly the memories of New York when I had just arrived—when helicopters used to land on the roof of the Pan Am Building and the gays were holding their first big demonstrations in Central Park. They are fragments that form a system, a language I talk to myself in. A language without words, if it's true that words are used to share one's thoughts with other people. Mr. Ceccarelli, the manager of the Stanic cafeteria, and Dr. Paoletti, the retired director, possess some scattered fragments of this language, but so few that when they utter them they sound like a scratched record, stuck for eternity on the same notes.

3

They were both at the cemetery, Mr. Ceccarelli and Dr. Paoletti, but with so many people there, I didn't have the time to talk to them as I would have liked.

So the next day, driving my mother's old Fiat, I went to Stagno to visit Mr. Ceccarelli, who had given me work in the cafeteria from the day my father died until I went back to school. He was older and more deaf.

"How's America?" he asked.

"So-so," I answered. Every time I go to see him, he asks the same question and I give him the same answer. He emerged from his kitchen, drying his hands on a white tea towel, and we went to sit at a table in the empty cafeteria.

"Is your work going well?" I asked.

"I'm satisfied," he said. "I have two Filipino girls now who do what you and your mother did. They're slow but very thorough. And you? When will you be returning to Italy?"

"To do what?"

"What you do there. Don't we have universities in this country? Haven't you been away from home long enough?" Even this was part of the script, like the last thing he said as I was leaving: "Have you been to see Dr. Paoletti?"

"I'm on my way there now."

Dr. Paoletti, for thirty years the executive director of the Stanic oil refinery and now retired, had been in his day a fanatic of haute cuisine. Unmarried and perhaps a homosexual, he had a house all draped in velvet and paved with marble; he held legendary dinner parties there for his friends. It was he who made it possible for me to go back to high school and later to university, paying my tuition fees, buying my books and, at Mr. Ceccarelli's suggestion, offering to take me on as his personal *chef de rang*. The work was fun for me and didn't interfere with my classes.

He still lived in town in the same eighteenth-century house with a dock on the canal and a great arched carriage entrance framed in *pietra serena*. It took me a half hour to drive through the beastly traffic from Stagno to Livorno, and another half hour to find a parking space. I walked up the D'Azeglio wharves for a hundred meters and thus fulfilled my pilgrimage of gratitude.

"Have you been to see Mr. Ceccarelli?" he asked.

"I've just come from there."

"I don't give dinner parties anymore. My few friends who aren't dead have problems with triglycerides, or cholesterol, or diabetes, or high blood pressure. I'm all right but everything tastes the same to me. How ironic: I cultivated the love of good food as one of the very few vices I could still enjoy in my old age. Mr. Ceccarelli sends one of his girls over every so often; they bring me small meals to put in the freezer. But not one of them is as intelligent as you were." That too is something he repeats every time. He had shrunk to a mere shadow. His voice too had changed.

"Maybe it's because I'm old and don't really desire anything anymore, but I think I'll never be keen on helping young people—male or female—get on with their studies. These days too many of them go to college anyway. The dumbest jackasses get a degree and then don't know what to do with it." That's what he told me and I'm afraid he was right. Then he added, "But you were something else. It was worth it, and you've proved that."

Before leaving, I dashed down to buy the ingredients I needed to prepare him a perfect *risotto alla milanese*—with beef marrow, onion, saffron, butter, parsley and lemon zest—cooked to just the right creaminess. I set the little table he always uses now, since he eats alone; but I moved it to the window, facing toward the sunset on the sea. The day was clear and the island of Gorgona was visible on the horizon. I used his splendid silver, his family crystal and china. I arranged the yellow roses I had bought in a Limoges vase. I sat him at the table and kissed him good-bye.

"You'll see, you'll enjoy this," I said, but I didn't believe it myself. I walked along the canal, thinking that maybe the next time I came to Italy Dr. Paoletti wouldn't be around anymore.

*   *   *

I stayed on for two days in those desolate rooms that had been my mother's home. It wasn't the farm house I had been brought up in; this was smaller, modern and dull. She had moved her things and herself there without much enthusiasm. The preserves she had continued to put up every summer were loaded into the Fiat and taken directly up to the eleventh floor of an anonymous high-rise apartment building in the city where my sister lived. There they stood, incongruously lined up on the shelves of her Scavolini kitchen in purple Formica: the sun-dried tomatoes, the bottle of olive oil with garlic cloves and hot peppers, the aubergine marinade, the pickled red onions.

In Mamma's house everything was clean and in perfect order, and yet those four rooms seemed never to have been lived in. I thought that perhaps my mother hadn't lived anywhere for years, from the time I had left for America and my sister had married. From that time her heart was not with her anymore, but half with me and half with Carmelina and her children.

I didn't even unpack the small bag I had brought with me. It was there sitting on a chair, as if I were staying in a hotel. From the window I couldn't see the country I remembered, but only the dismal suburbs that were gradually cementing together the beautiful old Tuscan cities and villages. I missed my New York apartment. I even missed all of you. I missed the Machine that was waiting for me on its cart next to my bed.

There was nothing left for me to do in Nugola. I had arrived too late to hold my mother's hand while she was dying. It was too late for everything. I called Alitalia to change to an earlier flight to New York.

Some play solitaire; for years I've played bridge by myself, every morning before going to work. I deal out the cards and play all the four players' hands, forcing each one not to remember his partner's or the opponents' cards.

The evening of the funeral, as I wandered unhappily from one room to another, I remembered I hadn't brought cards for my solitary morning bridge game. So before going to bed I went out to buy a deck at the local *caffé*.

That too had changed for the worse: plastic everywhere; new, indifferent owners; no one playing *tresette* at the tables. Only one thing was the same as in the old days: the cards they sold were not the bridge cards I always use, but the narrow ones they use to play *tresette*, made of cheap coated paper with grey backs. The numbers were not marked at the four corners, but just at the upper left and lower right.

I paid for the cards, walked around for a bit, and went home. I made myself a cheese omelette and went to bed early. From the open window I could hear the bitchy voice of a TV talk-show hostess.

She was saying, "What counts is keeping up your capacity for indignation."

She didn't need to be concerned. All her guests were indignant at each other and argued in very loud voices until the end of the show. Then a western came on and I finally fell asleep, lulled by the peaceful crackling of the Winchester 73s.

The morning after, I got up to make myself coffee and took it back to bed. When I opened North's hand to begin my morning bridge game, I couldn't see the numbers, because each upper left corner, except the last, was hidden by the overlapping card. That was strange, unless it was a faulty deck that had been printed in reverse. I thought about this later, while I was on the phone with Mr. Ceccarelli. I remembered that he kept the same kind of cards under the cash register at the cafeteria for the workers who played tresette during lunch break. I asked him to check out a deck.

"Upper left and lower right," he said. "There's nothing wrong with them. You're just holding them the wrong way."

That was when the question came to my mind, one that my mother more than anybody else could have answered. The telephone, same as in the old house, was in the kitchen: on the same sideboard, set at the same angle on the same neatly pressed doily, along with a picture of Pope John and the sewing basket. I recalled the day I brought home the first dress I had bought with my own money—pink linen with a square neckline. I was trying it on in front of the mirror in the bedroom I shared with Carmelina. She was sitting cross-legged on her bed, reading Mickey Mouse comics.

"It's too big in the waist," she declared. She was right.

I got the sewing basket and tried to alter the dress on my own without asking my mother for help. We used to split household chores among us. I helped Mother with the cooking and pickling, and I also took care of the garden and the chickens, did small carpenter jobs, and was the house electrician besides. But I had never done the laundry, the ironing, or the sewing. Even little Carmelina was better at all that than I was.

She had stopped reading and was looking at me with a critical eye. At a certain point she remarked, "You'll never get it right. It's taken you half an hour just to thread the needle because you're doing it backwards. And you are even sewing backwards."

So the thirty-year-old incident came back to me. A kind of symmetry of mind. I always try to instill in you a certain *esprit de géométrie*, as you know, and this is the right moment to apply it. The dicotyledonous theory—let's call it that—surfaces here and is immediately confirmed.

I said good-bye to Mr. Ceccarelli, hung up the phone, picked up the cards, and fanned them out so I could read the numbers. But it wasn't natural for me to hold them that way. So I tried holding the cards in my right hand and playing with my left; this way I could read the numbers, but it didn't work; it was as if my fingers were tied by invisible strings.

* * *

I called my sister to tell her I was leaving earlier. She didn't object.

"By the way," I ventured. It was useless, but I had to try.

"As far as you know, was I left-handed when I was small?"

"I can't say, really. I wasn't around when you were small. I have no idea."

"But would you say Mamma was the kind of person who would force me to use my right hand . . . to correct me if I were left-handed?"

That was a stupid question and Carmelina laughed.

"Would she? My dear, she was a peasant. She dressed in black. She went to mass every morning. She was the Rule personified. The quintessence of discipline and conformism. For her there was only one way to do things right, and any other way was wrong. You know that. You do the laundry on Mondays, you bake your bread on Fridays, you eat with your right, you write with your right, you cross yourself with your right, you cook eel for Christmas Eve and lamb for Easter. My Riccardo is left-handed, and I had a job trying to stop Mamma from tying his left hand into a bag so that he'd have to use his right."

"You mean Riccardo is left-handed?"

"Yes, and even the little one, I think. Right now, the only thing he knows how to do is suck his thumb, and he sucks his left one."

I thought this very significant.

"Isn't being left-handed an inherited trait?"

"I don't know. What's got into you, Martina?"

"Who would know whether I was left-handed or not?"

"Why is it so important to you?"

I didn't expect Carmelina to understand. She's cut all ties to her own childhood, let alone being interested in mine. But I insisted. "Come on, try to remember. Who could I ask?"

"No one. Our neighbors from those days are dead, except the Scheluccis. You might try to find them, they must be somewhere in America.

The Scheluccis, right. Marta Schelucci and her son Costantino. Keep them in mind because they're going to pop up again later.

What Carmelina said sounded incredible, almost sinister: I'm barely forty-two, and yet all the older ones are dead, apart from the Scheluccis, who are somewhere in America, but who knows where. To think that my mother asked them to find me an apartment in New York when I decided to leave Italy. When the building manager met me to hand over the keys, he also gave me their phone number. I didn't know area codes then, but thinking back, I believe it was a Long Island number. I remember calling right away to thank them. Mrs. Schelucci answered. I knew her husband had been killed in an accident at work a few years before. I was disappointed to learn that Costantino didn't live with her anymore. I imagined that he had gotten married, but I didn't want to ask. I called again a few times and promised to go see her, but I never did. It was one of those things you think about every once in a while but always keep putting off. Then I must have misplaced her number. If I had really wanted to find her in those first few years, I could have asked my mother. She had kept in touch with her for some time, but then, who knows. Some letters might have been returned . . . I don't know. Where to look for her? She could be dead. And Costantino, who knows where he wound up.

I packed the only thing that had a shadow of a memory about it, a terracotta jar with two small handles on the same side. The shape isn't Tuscan, and I've only seen it in our house, or in the houses of the other farmers who came from Lucania. Carmelina drove me to the airport. "Have you been to see Signor Ceccarelli and Dr. Paoletti?"

"Of course."

"They always talk about you. They're so proud of having helped a poor girl become a professor at an American university."

"They're two good souls." Thanks to them I hadn't become a professional cook, but instead one of the many Europeans stranded on the shores of numberless American universities. Usually in a teaching post where it's hard to get ahead, but where it only takes a single wave to knock you back, because that's America, and there they don't stand on ceremony. When the biggest customers—you tuition-paying students—lose interest, a course and sometimes a whole department can be eliminated, just like that.

4

I asked for an aisle seat. I could hear behind me the chatter of the other passengers and could easily figure out which were the occasional tourists—Americans on their way back from a European vacation, and Italians on a three-week, all-expenses-paid tour package, Disneyland and Niagara Falls included.

Then there were the commuters like me, dividing their time and their hearts. For some, both time and heart were split in half, as in my case; for others, perhaps doubled. Doubled because certain voices, certain faces—especially the ones I had seen in first class—seemed to belong to men and women who lived two perfectly functioning lives, one for each side of the Atlantic. I thought that very rich people had to get themselves at least two lives, to be lived in parallel, in order to enjoy all their belongings. Or maybe only one life, but boundlessly wide.

They were on a plane ferrying them through the six-hour time difference, as if they were merely walking from the terrace of their apartment on Via Giulia (with a view of the Tiber) to the sunken living room of their penthouse on Central Park South, without actually leaving the premises of their sacred property. As if the two locations were next to each other, unified by the sole fact of belonging to them, connected through the two opposite traffic flows: one illegal and westbound in dried *porcini* and the other legal and eastbound in miraculous vitamins in their giant white jars. As if they were granted extra time that allowed them to shift instantly from Europe to America and from yacht to log cabin, from wife to mistress, from big-game hunting in Uganda to a health farm at Marbella.

Call me Robinson. Given that in life we go from one shipwreck to the other, losing most or all of our possessions, each time forced to give up most or all of our privileges, habits, affections, and so on, I take some consolation—in both the small and big shipwrecks of life—in examining what I have left and seeing what can be made of it.

That's what happened when my handsome father, who used to play his guitar for us in the evenings and farm during the day, was crushed by his tractor. We were left on our own, with Carmelina barely ten and me just finishing grammar school.

My mother had begun wearing black from the time my father had taken us, her and me, just born, away from Lucania after our house was destroyed in one of the many earthquakes that strike that region. So when we buried Papa, she went to the cemetery dressed in her usual dress. After the funeral she sat down with us at the kitchen table and spoke to both of us, even to Carmelina who was only ten, in her usual tone of voice, just a little wearier, her face just a shade paler than usual. "Children," she said, "we'll have to figure something out."

We came up with an idea, she and I together, under Carmelina's tearful gaze. And when we tried it, it worked. We gave up running the farm because we knew that without Papa we'd never make it. Mamma wrote to the Scheluccis, in Lucania, friends of ours who had lost their house in a recent quake. We turned over half the house and the whole farm to them, keeping only a small vegetable garden and the chicken yard for ourselves.

Mamma got a job in the cafeteria at the Stanic oil refinery and convinced the manager, Signor Ceccarelli, to hire me as cook's helper even though I was only thirteen and a half. For two years we went down on foot to the highway every morning, even in cold weather, to catch the bus; and every day, even when the sun was beating down mercilessly, we'd walk home uphill from the bus stop.

Then, when Mamma could afford it, she bought a small Fiat and learned how to drive. After that we'd go to work—we said—like two Americans. I liked that life. We had our wages, our car, our vegetable garden, our chickens, our house. The Scheluccis supplied us with potatoes, wheat, and fruit, as if they were tenant farmers, even though we didn't have a written agreement and everything was based on our

word. They even used to watch Carmelina when we were at work, in the traditional solidarity that has enabled so many poor Italians to make their way better than others.

So call me Robinson. I almost like being shipwrecked so that I'll be forced to build myself a hut on a desert island. The present shipwreck was nothing; the only thing I missed was a bed to sleep in on my flight from Rome to New York. Luckily the two seats next to mine were empty, each with its neatly folded blanket and white pillow, sterilized and sealed in their plastic wrappers.

I pulled up both armrests and made a bed, first by padding the window side where I'd be laying my head. I used the three cushions, plus two of the blankets, and then wrapped myself in the third, like a tramp in Central Park. I fell into a sleep filled with the jumbled images of Nugola as it had been: the jars of artichoke hearts in oil lined up on the shelves I'd built for Mamma's pantry, the mulberry trees in the church square, the village doctor's house—a two-story cottage that was like an outpost overlooking the desolate landscape of Nugola Nuova, where begin the hills of solid gray clay that, unfertilized, won't nourish a tree, a bush, or even a single blade of grass. Only when doggedly cultivated will it yield—as far as the eye can see—fields of garlic plants as gray and dull as the soil they grow in.

On that side it gets beastly hot in summer, several

degrees hotter than in Nugola Vecchia, a difference that can be felt immediately on crossing the borderline. Just one step beyond the doctor's house, a matter of two feet, and everything changes—or used to change.

On our side of Nugola, the side favored by nature, there was Poggio di Mezzo with mushrooms growing in clusters under the shrubs of heather, the multicolored flash of the bee-eaters as they cut across the patches of sky one could see through the branches of the dense oaks. And Costantino Schelucci, two years older than me, with his long, tanned gypsy legs. He would pop out from the arbutus thicket, and without saying a word lift my short red skirt and begin my sexual education: a three-year course that lasted until he moved with his family to America.

Random, wandering images, useless for my work—which I couldn't do anyway without the help of the Machine, the quiet of my apartment, and the comfort of my bed.

With my legs and neck bent at ninety-degree angles, I lie there asleep for nine hours, immersed in chaotic dreams. Costantino comes back, this time sitting like an Arab with his legs crossed on the blackish moss of the Elephants' Ballroom, while I sit in the same position facing him, indifferent to the white panties outlining, under my red skirt, the dark bay between my thighs.

We're sharing a snack. There is the same intimacy and

trust between us as there was when we made love a moment earlier; the same as there will be when we make love a moment later. When we stand facing each other in the middle of the clearing and begin to undress, we're awed by a new discovery each time, grateful for the pleasure each enjoys and sure of the pleasure each will give back. He teaches me about his body and I teach him about mine, what little we know. We explore each other with our eyes, fingers, and tongues, but he solemnly agrees to 'respect' me, as we used to say with an expression already obsolete in those days. The meaning was that he had to refrain from trespassing on that sacred hymen, the location of which neither of us knew exactly. We both looked for it all the time, carefully, delicately, so as not to damage anything and to protect it from any careless move. But maybe something did happen we weren't aware of.

In fact, many years later, when I decided to offer that ultimate gift to the right man, the one I had saved it for, I didn't experience any of the phenomena I expected. Not the immense pain, not the sublime joy, not the bloody sheet, not the profound, immediate, and permanent transformation that was supposed to take place in my body and soul.

Unfortunately I can't insert this in a lecture, dear boys—and girls, especially. But then, I guess you know more than I do about the subject.

Anyway, this happened, or rather failed to happen—after

Costantino had already moved to America—on the torrid August day when Cesare and I decided to put an end to what changing social mores now deemed an embarrassing condition for a twenty-two-year-old girl. I felt neither pain nor pleasure. Trying not to be noticed, I kept peeking under the sheets but didn't see any blood stains. As to the transformation that would make a woman of me, it simply didn't happen. I would look in the mirror and keep seeing the same black-haired girl—a girl and not a woman—during our engagement and the two fruitless years of our marriage.

Between one dream and another I slept until the flight attendant woke me with the usual steaming white facecloth. Below me lay the incomparable beauty of Manhattan.

5

I had the taxi drop me off a block from my place and stopped at Mrs. Califano's deli. She sent mineral water and food items up to me every two weeks. I left her an order for the next delivery, and to eat that night bought some robiola cheese, arugula, a bagel, and a small package of fresh tagliatelle. I went by the dry cleaner's to pick up my green skirt and jacket. Loaded down with my valise, groceries, and dry cleaning, I dived into the air of my beloved city.

I'm so used to the smell of New York that I almost don't sense it anymore. But I find it again and so keenly every time I come back from Italy. I manage to single out its components, even to estimate the percentage of each, which varies from area to area. The ethnic cuisines, with their own special spices, one in particular with a strange human aroma, like stale sweat, or urine. Yet, incredibly, not as disgusting as one would imagine. And garlic, pepperoni, hamburger, french fries. Herbal and vegetable aromas, including marijuana. What has disappeared, oddly, is the smell of cigarette smoke. The few who still smoke do it secretly; one can't see or sense them.

Powerful, more than any other smell, is broccoli. *Broccoli uber Alles*. The city's air-exchange pumps, air conditioners, fans are all clogged with broccoli fumes, accumulated year after year. It must be something like what cholesterol does to arteries. The broccoli smell must harden in greenish plaques in the elbows of air ducts. It took only six months to clog the pipelines of my fabulous condo. The air in the halls, which are lined in aristocratic sage-colored fabric, and in the brass and mahogany elevators is constantly steeped in that smell.

Then the steam coming from the vents in the streets. This too has its peculiar door. At Fifty-seventh and Lexington there is a small hole in the asphalt, right in the middle of the street, which shoots its brave little jet straight up several feet even when the weather is windy and the steam clouds from the official vents disperse as soon as they reach the surface.

And the smell of bed sheets, towels, shirts, all of the New York laundry, that for its entire lifetime is never allowed to dry in the sun or even in the open air. A faint but disgusting smell. Something that is probably noticed only by us who've recently arrived from poorer countries, afflicted by the sight of windows draped with drying laundry, but rewarded by the fresh smell of really clean sheets.

I'm used to the smells of New York. I'm moved when I find them waiting for me on my return. Among the unforgivable ones I would only put the cloying scent of perfumed candles— an incomprehensible affectation in so many houses—one of the worst smells, beaten only by the heady potpourris of dried flowers, apples, cinnamon and obnoxious sandalwood that engulf one on entering those shops that sell sophisticated, overpriced housewares: gilt corkscrews, frying pans of unmanageable weight, pepper grinders in the shape of Longobard towers, plates, blankets, tablecloths in assorted precious colors on scrupulously natural pine shelves.

I entered my building under the benevolent eye of the doorman, Mr. Serrano, went past the tropical garden in the lobby, boarded the elevator—uneasily as usual—and was shot up to the thirty-second floor. At three in the afternoon, local time, I was on my terrace watering my herbs, which though droopy had managed to survive.

I had lived in the same apartment building at the corner of Fifty-third and Ninth for fifteen years. When the building was demolished to be replaced by a much bigger one I wasn't left homeless; the management sent me a polite note with an offer of another apartment about the same size and price as my old one. It was in a newly built high-rise on East Thirty-eighth Street at the river.

When I moved into my new one bedroom on the thirty-second floor, the building was still almost empty and many of the apartments unfinished. But the doorman's desk was set up already—a stainless steel wonder, the cockpit of a spaceship. Between this bit of science fiction and the elevators was a small lake, stocked with colossal goldfish and surrounded by lianas, palms, and tree ferns. I was impressed by the exotic lobby, by the breathtaking view I had from my windows. I couldn't believe it wasn't costing me more than the modest old place on West Fifty-third.

I was so cowed by such elegance that I considered donating my furniture to the Salvation Army and buying all new. Eventually I was courageous, or stingy, enough not to do it. I brought over my pots of basil and rosemary, thyme and calamint, marjoram and chives, dill and sage. I also brought my old furniture, no matter if, like my little herb garden, it was far below the standards of the flashy condominium.

After I had finished watering the plants, I pressed the play button on the answering machine: a university colleague inviting me to dinner; Magnolia Washington, with her black-velvet voice, reminding me of the address of the off-Broadway theater where she'd be singing in a couple of weeks; the carpenter telling me my bookcase was ready.

Magnolia worked for a phone company and wrote her own songs, accompanying herself on the piano. Every now and then she got hired to do a TV commercial. Recently she had dubbed a talking potato in an ad for Idaho Crunchies.

The carpenter was in reality a Bulgarian writer who came to America after an adventure-laden escape two years before the fall of the Berlin Wall. As a carpenter he left much to be desired. He knew Eugene Onegin by heart but didn't have the vaguest idea of how to use a square or a level.

I also knew a former stage actor, an Italian—handsome, distinguished, with gray hair—who worked as mâitre d´ in a posh restaurant. I think he was good at what he did because he played, evening after evening, Lawrence Olivier's role in an old sentimental black-and-white movie. He wore his tux like a stage costume, and with each performance he tried to add something to the great actor's interpretation. He made a lot of money and enjoyed himself.

New York is a city where people come to do one thing and wind up doing another. Or hope to do something and succeed at nothing. Or disappear from one day to the next. I know a woman who bakes very good cakes. Almost every year in her native Wrightsville, Oklahoma, before she moved to New York, she used to win first prize in the cheesecake contest at the annual cattle fair. Now she's putting away a tidy sum making cakes. She makes them in her kitchen, about twenty a day. It's a recent activity: she used to teach mathematics in Brooklyn. One night she was mugged, right inside the school—beaten, robbed, and raped and then locked in a storage room. It was one of those huge school buildings where anything can happen and nobody is very surprised. She wasn't either, but she decided it wouldn't happen again. She changed her life, changed work from one day to the next. Now she never leaves home. She orders flour, sugar, and the other ingredients she needs from a wholesaler by phone. A boy picks up her cakes every morning and takes them around to her customers. Once a week she gets a delivery of cardboard boxes bearing her trademark in blue florid characters: *The Math Teacher's Pies.*

She plays the violin. She has a collection of Murano paperweights. When I visit her she opens the door a couple of inches with the chain on and makes sure nobody is behind me. We have tea together with a slice of one of her legendary cakes.

I put on my track suit and went up to the top floor to work out for a half hour at the health club, which offers hope of eternal youth to us lucky tenants at Turtle Bay Tower. I started out on the Run-oo, set to three. The machine is located in front of the windows. Three blocks to the south the helicopter from the airport was making its vertical descent. I kept puffing on the treadmill until the chopper took off again with its ear-splitting roar. Then I did the Magic Lift and Abdo-Trim. Just as I was leaving, Jerry Keleti arrived. He lives in 32E, next door to my 32D. "Welcome home, dearie," he said. I told him about my mother and he hugged me.

Jerry makes a living working as a translator, but he is really a glottologist. Years ago, when he still hoped for an academic career, he lived six months in the extreme north of Alaska to study the language of an Eskimo tribe that was by then almost extinct. In fact the language was known only by two persons, who were cousins and—because of family quarrels—were not on speaking terms. There were no conversations Jerry could tape. During an endless winter he had to sleigh across a chilly plain from one end to the other in order to extract from the rival cousins few unfriendly grunts: the last rattle of a dying language.

After his book came out, Jerry started to work as a translator in order to stay warm and never eat mackerel again.

He keeps rigid, strange hours. He gets up at three in the morning and works until nine, when he goes up to the health club to exercise for half an hour. When he gets back to his apartment, the hall is immediately permeated by the smell of the goulash he's reheating in his microwave. He eats his very early lunch—weather permitting—on his terrace, where I can see him sitting at a small, neatly set table. There's a yellow vase with flowers on it, and a stereo plays background music, always the same pieces: the Trout Quintet with Clifford Curzon, Janet Baker singing "*Divinités du Styx*," or the duet from Semiramide with Horne and Sutherland.

At ten-thirty his afternoon begins, dedicated to reading, housekeeping, shopping. At three he goes back to the health club for a few minutes, then shuts himself in with a bottle of whiskey and a large bag of potato chips to watch a videotape, after which he goes to bed with a book.

I know which movies he watches because he told me,

and also because the partitions between apartments are thin. I know them by heart: *Rio Lobo*, *Man's Favorite Sport*, *Bringing Up Baby*, and a few others. I know he watches intently until a line comes up that's in all his favorite films. "Are you crazy?" asks Jane (or Paula or Katherine). The words might change but the meaning's the same and always sends the same thrill up his spine. Cary (or Rod or John) has just pulled a boner, but the woman knows how to handle the ineptitude, the weakness, the helplessness of the human male without making a big thing of it. Indeed, she not only forgives him for his bumbling behavior, but she acknowledges it as a special charm.

Katherine, Irene, Paula, Jane—his favorites, elegant, self-confident, a little bossy, superlatively tart—say to him "Are you crazy" and mean, instead "You know, sweety, the fool things you always say and do, and those horn-rimmed glasses you wear, and that silly look of yours, are so endearing. Do leave everything to me. Let me spoil you. Let me seduce you. And don't worry about it: the stupider you are, the more I like you." Jerry looks a little like Cary Grant and is proud of it.

Even the books he reads before he falls asleep are almost always the same ones. Picking one of them from the pile on his night table is for him like entering a familiar place to spend the evening with a fascinating woman—Elizabeth Bennet, Anna Karenina, Mathilde de la Mole, the Princess

Casamassima. As his eyes close, the words continue to run through his head, coming from his memory rather than from the page.

He is a habitual customer at the Hungarian restaurant on the next block, where he is always given the same table. He has dinner there once a week; sometimes he invites me, sometimes some other girl with whom—he lets me under-stand—his relationship is less platonic.

Sometimes I can get him to come to dinner, and he's happy to: he's fond of me and likes my cooking. But I have to adapt to him because he couldn't adapt to me or to the rest of the world. I skip lunch and make an afternoon meal for us of fish soup *alla Livornese*, or Lucanian meatballs, which we have at four with a bottle of the Hungarian wine he brings. At five-thirty the party ends; I give him a gentle shove in the direction of his apartment. Sometimes I lead him to his door and help him with the key. I've never put him to bed, but I'd do it willingly if it were necessary. It's true he often gets drunk in the afternoon, but during the evening, in the com-pany of his beloved ghosts, he's totally regenerated, and the morning after he appears fresh and rested, witty, intelligent, clean-shaven, and innocent.

You didn't expect me back at school for another two days, but I went anyway to pick up my mail. I spent a couple of hours at the library, then I went to my office to fill out some forms I had been putting off for days. At five I made another pot of coffee in the electric coffee maker I keep in the office. From the window I could see the thick row of golden mums in front of the entrance to the history department. I kept the door open and a few of you stopped in to talk. You noticed, I think, that I was glad to see you. Incredibly enough, I miss you when I'm away for a while.

Evening came in a moment. I was in the subway at half past six and by seven I was lying in my beautiful porcelain bathtub imported from Italy, basking in water that was softened and perfumed by a few drops of an expensive bath oil Jerry Keleti had given me for Christmas. The stereo was softly playing Haydn's Turkish minuet.

You know, I take loving care of myself; I'm a real spinster in this respect. The bath I take after I get home at night is a kind of lustral rite, a purification ceremony that allows me to leave unwanted thoughts on my doormat.

I leaned my head on the rim of the tub and closed my eyes. My mother was dead. I let the tears flow, for the first time since I saw her in her coffin. Then I took the rough hemp glove she had crocheted for me and rubbed my whole body until it turned pink.

I'd found a message in Italian on the answering machine: "It's ten a.m. My name is Cerignola. I'll try again earlier tomorrow morning."

I had never met anybody by that name, yet the voice sounded familiar.

I made myself *tagliatelle* with pesto and took it along with a glass of red wine to the living room. I turned on the TV just in time to catch the Italian news. By nine I was in bed, the Machine set up for a night of dreaming.

Tuesday: Lobster Armoricaine

I

First a rasping sound, neither music nor noise, then a whisper: "You're Italian but you live in New York. You're forty-two. This is my voice: yours. Tell our dream."

Without opening my eyes, still half-asleep, I began to speak. After ninety seconds of silence the Machine understood I had nothing more to say and stopped recording. "Your breakfast will be ready in a couple of minutes," it said. "You'll have to be in class in an hour and a half to teach your course in European history. Have a good day."

I floated back to the world, while the coffee—the watery American kind I've come to like—perked through the electric pot connected to the Machine. Two frozen croissants were warming in the toaster oven. I took my time over breakfast, enjoying the morning light on the East River and listening to the dream I had recorded a few minutes before and already forgotten.

* * *

I am in a car, sitting next to Mariarosa Romiti. The car is speeding down a steep, narrow road, swerving on hairpin curves along a cliff's edge. The purple, stormy sea below throws off a smell of pines and salt. Since Mariarosa is one of the clumsiest people I've ever known, I am relieved to observe that I am sitting on the left. "Thank God," I say to myself, "this means I'm driving."

Night had delivered a new message, going back to the dicotyledonous theory. Do you follow me? Never mind. Maybe later.

When I finished a second croissant and a third mug of coffee, I put the tray on the Machine, spread my knees under the covers to form a flat triangle in front of me, and took a deck of cards from the night table. As I shuffled the cards I reminded myself—as I often do—that I should have installed a small pull-out game table in the Machine. It would have been a minor technical problem compared to the ones I had to solve to put together the electronics.

I cut the deck twice. I knew the four piles had thirteen cards each without even counting, just as I know the right amounts of the ingredients for the dishes I cook without using measuring spoons.

North opened with one heart, East answered with one spade and the bid closed with five clubs from South, who failed the contract by one trick. I told you I play bridge by myself every morning, scrupulously bidding each player's hand and literally forgetting what the other players are holding. Played this way, bridge is not so much an exercise in logic as in morals: I've dedicated myself to it for years with the same seriousness as when I work out on the Maxi-cam machine at our penthouse health club. An exercise in de-identification and reidentification as someone else: certainly an elementary exercise, but I felt it was essential for me to play it everyday. It allowed me to think of myself in the third person. Martina Satriano is back in New York after burying her mother. Now there's no one to knit sweaters for her. Now her phone won't ring at three in the morning and a voice ask if she was frightened during the hurricane. And she won't answer sleepily, "The hurricane is in Florida, Mamma, two thousand kilometers from here. Like from your house to Oslo."

Playing every day for and against myself, taking the role of each player, was a great system, till that moment. I needed the Machine for scientific work, but it was the bridge game that detached me, that allowed me a view from the outside. Until that day. Now certain parameters had changed; the morning bridge game seemed irrelevant, destined to become a mere pastime.

I was hired to teach European history, not exactly my ~~⸝ference~~. I soon discovered, however, that European histo- ~~includes~~ almost anything, you just have to stretch it a bit. ~~⸝om~~ then on my courses became quite popular because I ~~⸝ased~~ them on catchy themes, such as "Sin in Greco-Roman Culture," "Catholic Ethics and Capitalism," "Right and Left in the Nazi-Fascist Movements," "Identity and Belonging." Sometimes, while I was lecturing, I felt I was walking dangerously close to the brink of nonsense. At times I definitely went over the edge. On the other hand, it seemed pointless to revisit the same concepts that had been agreed on for ages. How could I in all decency stand at a lectern to repeat—at a hundred dollars an hour—that I'm against war, racism, exploitation? Who would ever assert the contrary? I'd feel as if I were stealing my salary, babbling such platitudes. I'd rather explore logical quicksand, come what might.

You bore with me, usually. Some courses were more successful than others. Some were taken mostly by boys, others mostly by girls. The course I was teaching then, "The Biblical Concept of Neighbor in Italian Culture," was not among the popular ones. About twelve students, girls and boys, sat there waiting for me.

"As we've already said," I began, "The Italian word for the biblical meaning of neighbor, *prossimo*, comes from the Latin word *proximus*, which means 'the closest'. Not just close, but closer evidently than analogous individuals are.

2

The telephone rang at eight-thirty while I w
cards away. I still felt the voice wasn't unfamiliar,
connect a face with it.

"Professor Martina Satriano? Forgive my
early, but I'm here in New York for just a few da
absolutely must talk to you before I leave. My n
Cerignola, Sebastiano Cerignola."

Oh, I thought, *that* Cerignola. Now I understood
the voice had seemed familiar. But I couldn't imagine what
author of *The Samson Syndrome* and *The Flat Line* could ev
want from me.

"Professor Sebastiano Cerignola? I've read your books.
And when I'm in Italy, I sometimes watch you on television."

"And I've read your monograph on Lorenzo da Ponte's
years in America. And the one on masculine identity.
Excellent works."

That was odd. My slim books, published by a university press, had had limited sales, and then only in the United
States.

"I must talk to you. To begin with, could you give me
a couple of hours of your time?" I was curious. We made an
appointment for six that evening. "I'll meet you at the bar at
the Crystal Room," he said.

We've seen how difficult and sensitive measuring this proximity can be, since it is not an absolute value but rather a matter of comparative distance. Therefore, who is my proximus: the one I find actually closer at the present moment, or the one who is closer to me in my heart, the one I was originally given as closer, the one who's been closer to me the longest, the one who's been closer in trying circumstances, or someone else?

"Now I'll propose a further consideration. To determine whether A or B is closer to C, we have to know the positions of A and B, but for heaven's sake, also the position of C."

The students looked puzzled. I went to the blackboard, printed a few letters and drew some random lines, which made little sense even to me.

"How can we compare A's and B's distance from C if we're not sure where C is, or more important, what C is, or if C is there at all? Can you tell me where C is, or even where I am, or each one of us is?"

I put down the chalk and went back to my desk. I went on with the lecture, trying to stay within the subject. I would have liked to continue by saying, "Because if we have within us something like an indivisible center of gravity, which is not "I think," "I speak," "I believe," "I vote," but simply "I am;" if that's so—as I believe it is—what precisely is this thing in my case? Is this minuscule particle of light from Lucania, or from Tuscany, or from New York? Is this shred of identity right- or left-handed? The volcanic mountains of Lucania trembled hard enough to destroy my father's house at the same time a Tuscan landowner went bankrupt and was selling his land for a few liras a hectare: was this the will of almighty Destiny, or a casual detour from the predictable course of events? And was it in my cards that my marriage wouldn't work, that I wouldn't have children, that I wouldn't conform to a pattern of life in Italy I could have built a future on? Or was my inner self put off track when I was a baby and my mother stopped me from reaching out for food with my left hand the first time? And so should I locate point C, from which I must begin measuring to determine the comparative distances of points A and B, where it is now, or where it should have been? And since I'm having trouble understanding where it is—in Lucania, or Tuscany, or New York City, or on the thirty-second floor connected to the Machine—and what it is—farmer's daughter, *chef de rang*, university teacher—how can I possibly determine whether it is right- or left-handed?"

Would you have understood me? Possibly. I know that adopted children, no matter how happy and loved, feel the need at a certain age to search for the person who would have been their mother had the course of events not been arbitrarily changed. I just wanted to know who I would have been if the course of events hadn't been changed. Would you have thought it so stupid? If I had had a twin sister and had been separated from her, wouldn't it be logical that I would try to find her? And if that twin lived in my own body, isn't it even more justifiable to want to know what happened to her?

3

I would have liked to say all this, but I didn't. I don't know exactly what I did say, because while I spoke I was thinking about my appointment at the Crystal Room. In my twenty years here no one had ever invited me to that temple of the American Dream, much less a famous sociologist who admired my books. I spent the day in a trance, mechanically performing my usual tasks, my mind fixed on two questions that I still didn't know how interrelated would prove to be: "Am I truly myself?" and then: "Whatever does Professor Cerignola want from me?"

I reviewed in my mind the dream, the dirt road winding dizzily down the cliff. The stormy sea was obviously Italian. That smell in the salt air—so brisk, so pungent—can only be sensed near a smaller sea, worn out and condensed by a long history. The road, on the contrary, couldn't be in Italy. Our territory is by now almost entirely covered by asphalt; curves and hills and valleys are leveled by thousands of tunnels and viaducts, especially along the coasts, which are now all overdeveloped, urbanized. The road resembled rather the dusty ribbon that uncoils from Arizona down to Monument Valley, the most typical American landscape, the postcard scene best known after the Manhattan skyline with the Empire State and Chrysler Buildings. I had driven that road only once, sitting next to Magnolia Washington in a rented car during a holiday in Arizona and Utah. She was driving, and I was more than happy to close my eyes whenever I was feeling unbearably acrophobic. In my dream, though, I had been glad to be driving and didn't fear heights at all.

So, would the left-handed me have driven my life instead of letting it drive me? And would I have managed to be in Italy and in USA at the same time, enjoying the best of both? Sure, if I had got myself a teaching job in an Italian university, I would have taught American literature. No one could have kept me away from Emily Dickinson or Henry James, nor from my contemporaries, Philip Roth and John Updike.

Would I have stayed in Italy, and would I have enjoyed friends as caring and intelligent as Magnolia and a life as open and natural as Monument Valley? And what about love? In the dream, the subject did not arise.

I"m sorry to say I didn't give my work much attention that day. The subway, the university corridors, the class, your faces, my sandwich at one, my study, the mail, the subway back—everything seemed to be condensed into a very short dream.

I left a little earlier than usual and went home to shower and change. At 6:01, my green suit and I emerged from the elevator into the thirty-ninth floor of the Crystal Room. A maître d' came up to me wearing the mournful expression of an undertaker. I mumbled my name and told him I was probably expected. He bowed and solemnly asked me to follow him.

The professor stood up and kissed my hand. He was shorter and thinner than he seemed on television. He had already ordered a whiskey sour for himself and one for me. We sat down, and then he asked me the same question I'm always asked by the cafeteria manager at the refinery in Livorno: "What do you think of America?"

I took a sip of my drink while I tried to come up with an answer.

"I came back the day before yesterday," I said finally, "after a few days in Italy. And while the plane was landing I told myself, 'Here I am, back home.' I looked down at Manhattan and was delighted that it was still there to greet me."

"What about Italy? What do you think about when your plane is landing there?"

"Italy . . . Italy is like a close relative. No one moves me or irritates me or touches me the way my father or my mother did, or the way my sister and her children do . . . "

I began to tell him about Nugola Vecchia, about the ugly building boom, about the funeral, about the help I got from Signor Ceccarelli and Dr. Paoletti when I was a child. I went on and on because he seemed to be taking in my every word, and if I paused he put me back on track with a pointed question.

At seven-thirty we were still there, and I still couldn't understand what Professor Cerignola wanted from me.

New York gleamed beneath us. I took a pistachio from the black crystal bowl an assistant undertaker had brought to the table.

". . . it's because I never drink hard liquor," I said. "If I talk too much, stop me."

"Don't worry. Tell me if you'd like to go back to Italy."

I felt like thinking of myself in the third person. Martina Satriano is sitting at a table in the Crystal Room with Professor Cerignola. He seems about to offer her a job in Italy.

"You can't begin a new career at forty-two. In Italy I'd have to start from zero. And I'd stay at zero, just as I would have if I hadn't had the good sense to leave."

"I wouldn't have come this far to ask you to begin from zero . . . Imagine being in a very prestigious position."

Professor Cerignola needs an assistant. Martina Satriano is not about to fall for it, I thought. I shook my head.

"Listen, I've tried, in Italy. And I didn't make it. I didn't have social standing, I didn't have money, I wasn't a Catholic, I wasn't a communist. Who could ever have got ahead under those conditions? Perhaps if I had been a genius, and mind you, only perhaps. You know our country, locked into cabals, mafias, families, political parties . . . The loners don't get ahead."

The professor nodded. There was an encouraging smile on his face. I went on.

"Maybe if I'd have become a cook, I'd be the manager of the Danieli kitchen, but, you see, I wanted to impress my mother, Dr. Paoletti, Mr Ceccarelli . . . They all thought it was a crime if a bright girl like me didn't get a degree and go on to an academic career. I'm not sure if I did what I wanted or what they wanted."

4

While I was talking he'd ordered *lobster armoricaine* for both of us. Before I started on mine, I finished my second whiskey sour. I don't know why; I certainly didn't like it. "Sometimes," I said, "I think all the answers are in the Machine."

"In the Machine?"

I had been going on and on. As long as I was telling him everything about me, I might as well tell him about the Machine.

"It's a complicated piece of equipment. I built it with the help of a very good Turkish technician who has a store on Forty-second Street. The main part is a device that's sold everywhere under various brand names; mine is called the Dream Machine. It's supposed to help you drop off to sleep and wake up in a good mood. It has prerecorded messages—possibly even subliminal stuff, so they say. More likely it's just one of those traps for gadget-lovers. At the beginning I only used it as a timer, connecting it to a coffee maker and to a toaster oven for croissants. Breakfast would be prepared automatically every morning and I would have it while I was in bed looking out over the river . . . Then I connected other things to it: sleep-making music, special sounds for drifting awake, an alarm for snapping awake. Then I added messages for self-hypnosis, commands for posthypnosis . . . "

"And what," the professor asked, "was the purpose of the new version?"

Along with the lobster they brought a dry white from Gorizia. I drank a glass and it made up for the whiskey sour.

"In the beginning—after the second modification—I just used it to remember my dreams. The self-hypnosis program started at night ten minutes after I turned off the light. And the next morning came the posthypnotic command to retell the dream, preceded by a sound that acts as a perfect bridge, you see? It has the power to bring me back to a state of partial consciousness without cutting me off from the mystery of the dreams. I reach the threshold of reality bringing with me all the magic of the other world. I recount the dream without being fully awake. The sound is the voices of the dead, the voices of the stones, an echo from the depths of time."

"The voices of the stones?" repeated the professor.

"The stones, the desert. The dark side, the secret side. An incredibly arcane sound."

The professor was lost. "I see" he said feebly.

"It's just a short piece on a recording that anyone can get hold of. I taped it off a video called *The Return to the Red Desert*."

"I'm not familiar with it."

"It wasn't very successful, I think. It's not very good. But of all the Australian movies, it has the best sound track for getting a clean recording of that music."

"That music?"

"Yes, it's part of aboriginal folklore. A harsh, panting sound . . . You must have heard it. It's in Peter Weir's early movies . . . You can find it in almost all Australian movies . . . I don't even know what it's called or what kind of instrument produces it. You might very well ask why I didn't research it, but, you see, I'm not interested in knowing what kind of gourd or reed or animal skull the sound comes from. To the contrary, I'd rather not know. I put it into the Machine precisely because it so clearly belongs to another order of things, to another level of reality. The less I know, the better, you understand. The spell is stronger if the details are fewer. So first we have the aboriginal sound, then the posthypnotic command to recount the dream. The idea was to maintain awareness of the dreams and bring them to light without trying to impose logic on them. Then I began thinking the thing could work in both directions . . . I thought I might be able to take a bit of consciousness into my sleep—my daytime thought mode, let's call it—that would compel me to memorize those happy insights that come to us in our dreams and bring them with me to the light of morning. It was supposed to be a kind of bridge between sleep and waking, but a guarded bridge that could only be crossed by what was good and useful, while the monsters would be kept at bay . . . "

"How did you achieve this?"

"I changed the evening messages. I added the recorded dream from the previous night."

"Did it work?"

"Not really. But well enough to realize I couldn't stop there. My dreams had taken on so much life that the next step seemed inevitable. Why, I asked myself, do we say that reality is reality and dreams are dreams? Who's to tell me that what I see and hear and touch now—the lobster, the wine from Gorizia, you, professor—is more real than the dream I had last night? If I asked you, 'Tell me, Professor Sebastiano Cerignola, are you really real?' you'd answer yes, but who's to say I can trust you? Wouldn't Mariarosa Romiti, whom I dreamt about last night, have given me the same answer to the same question? And the smell of the Mediterranean I smelled in my dream was as pleasant as the bouquet of this wine and just as convincing."

"And so?"

"And so I became aware of something obvious that's there for all to see, but no one ever notices, and certainly no one ever pointed out to me. The only difference between so-called reality and so-called dream is that our days are linked to one another by memory, while our nights are not. I know today what happened yesterday and the day before. The other day, yesterday, and today are bridged by memory, thus forming a continuity. Each day begins where the preceding one ended. In tonight's dream, on the contrary, everything will begin from the beginning. There won't be anything left of last night's dream. The next episode will not begin, like in a serialized soap opera, from the moment when Mariarosa and I are hurtling in a white Fiat down a road on the edge of a stormy sea. I won't remember that this ever happened. I'll be who knows where, with who knows whom, involved in who knows what adventure, which won't retain a trace of the preceding one."

"I see," the professor said. "Whatever's linked by memory is real and whatever's divided into separate episodes isn't."

"Exactly. But doesn't it seem too weak a criterion to define the limits of reality by? It lacks the mathematical rigor that demands compelling and exhaustive criteria. This is neither one or the other. How will we consider a case of amnesia? Do we claim that after a blow on the head you exit from reality? And how do we consider recurring dreams, when there is a glimmer of memory between one dream and another? This way of denying reality to dreams isn't based on rigor but on simple, petty, antiphilosophical common sense. We say: 'It's obvious that reality is reality and dreams are dreams.' 'But why?' 'Well, because that's the way it is.' You must admit that if we're satisfied with such shoddy logic on such an important issue, there's nothing in all decency left to do but let all philosophy go out of business and defer to Poor Richard's practicalities. We should resign ourselves to the notion that the only measure of reality is common sense."

"I sometimes think that wouldn't be such a bad idea."

"Oh, please." I had almost finished my pilaff and was about to tackle the lobster. Dr. Paoletti was allergic to lobster, so I had never cooked or tasted one.

It didn't seem that great: sweet and stringy.

"We'd be in quite a fix if we relied on common sense," I said. "Common sense is petty, intolerant, presumptuous. It's the acrobatics of reason that assure us *liberté*, *egalité*, and *fraternité*."

He was picking out the meat from the shell with superlative agility.

"And so you created a reserve reality for yourself, thanks to your machine?"

"No, but I'm working on it. It will be the theme of my next book. And the further along I get, the more I view our daytime reality, the chain of days linked together by memory, with greater detachment. It's only half our existence. The other half, the hidden half, is so close . . . one needs only to reach out in the dark. I can't understand why I started telling you these things. It's only because I have tremendous confidence in this work. The Machine has been my entire life for two years."

"That's not so good," Professor Cerignola said. "A good-looking young woman like you shouldn't have a machine as a significant other."

I took it as a compliment, but didn't acknowledge it.

I was having trouble with the gilded claw crackers the head undertaker had brought me.

"Getting control of this beast is not easy," I observed.

The professor smiled. He had a pleasing face, dark-skinned, with a beak of a nose like Pulcinella's. "You're using the wrong hand," he said. "Try the other one." Then he added, "Unless you're left-handed."

I put down the cracker and drank another glass of wine. "It's unbelievable how things pile up like this," I said.

"I beg your pardon?"

"I mean . . . for years we don't think about a certain long-lost school friend, let's say; then one morning we hear his name mentioned, in the afternoon we come upon a photograph, and the next day we run into him. It happens to everybody and we have to admit it's rather strange. The other day I began thinking I'm a repressed lefty, and here you are, noticing that I do certain things backwards. And then the dream I had last night . . . "

I told him about my nocturnal drive with Mariarosa. "You see, the right side, the left side; intelligence, instinct; the domineering side, the dominated side . . . "

He looked puzzled. Then he tried to go back to his point.

"The fact is that things have changed a lot in Italy. You could, in a certain sense, be placed in the position you would have had if things hadn't been so . . . closed when you graduated from university. Forget about dreams; this could be reality."

"Oh, but dreams do matter, believe me," I said. "Everything hangs together in proper order."

He smiled and indicated with a nod that if it really mattered so much he'd go along with me and my nonsense.

"Don't think I haven't read the Italian papers these last few years," I went on. "Don't think I haven't thought the things you want me to think. I know this might be just the right moment for me to reconsider everything in my life, including the wrongs I've suffered, the failures, the loneliness . . . and even the dreams. The reality of my dreams might be my left-handed reality . . . the other hypothesis, the one that hasn't taken place. The woman I would have become if they'd allowed me to use my left hand."

I squinted to bring him into focus. "You know, I probably should talk to you about my father."

By now he realized that I had had too much to drink and had learned to adjust quickly to my spotty logic. So he nodded with the solemn air of a priest hearing confession.

"Yes, do."

"My father was a farmer who became an engineer on the railroads and ran engines on the Potenza-Foggia line. And then he lost his house in an earthquake and suffered a head injury that blinded him totally in one eye and seven-tenths in the other. So he took his severance pay, bought a piece of land in Tuscany, and went back to farming. He could recite *The Divine Comedy* by heart, but he'd learned how to read on his own without ever having gone to school. The grammar school certificate he used to apply for the job on the railroad he got by studying at home, after work, when he was twenty-two. He had his own way of expressing himself, partly like an ignorant farmer and partly like a fourteenth-century humanist."

"That's beautiful, in the old tradition . . . "

I interrupted him. "I remember the elections, the first ones I can recall. I must have been about ten. In the days just before voting time everyone in our village had got terribly worked up and angry with one another, even to the point of violence. I was upset by this climate of hostility among people who were bound by old ties of friendship. Especially between the blacksmith and the owner of the bull-stud service; for years they had played cards every night at the *caffè*, and now they couldn't even sit down at the table without arguing. So I asked my father which of them was right, Volpini or Corridoni."

The professor waited a minute, expecting me to go on, then asked, "What did your father say to that?"

I thought about it for a moment. Now it no longer seemed that what I was trying to say could be expressed in the words my father used that night. In fact, I didn't remember them that well myself.

I said, "You know, I really couldn't repeat what he said exactly. And even if I could, word for word, it wouldn't have the same meaning. We were in the stable and he was sitting on a three-legged stool, milking a cow. It was a summer night smelling of manure and hay . . . the words sounded different than they would here."

I looked around the restaurant. "Here they might not seem so memorable. Essentially he counseled me to assume everyone's in good faith, especially people who have different opinions from mine. Then he talked to me about parallax."

"Parallax?"

"Yes. A farmer from Lucania, sitting on a milking stool, talked to his ten-year-old daughter about parallax. I don't know where he even got the word from. Maybe from the science page of a newspaper. What I find so extraordinary is how he turned it into a metaphor that became the basis for his simple, candid moral philosophy. He asked me, 'Do you know what parallax is?' 'No,' I answered. 'It's simple,' he said. 'It's the distortion of space due to a shift in the point of view. I look up at the cow from this position and she almost covers my whole field of vision and seems to be all udders. If I stand up and walk over to the feeding trough, she doesn't take up my field of vision anymore and therefore is smaller, and furthermore has a nose, eyes, and horns.'

"In short, professor, I don't know how to tell the story the way I'd like to, but that night my father taught me to doubt any absolute truth. He showed me—speaking with his heart, not with his mind—that at the bottom of every Absolute Truth, of every unshakeable opinion, there is a mean little bad faith, busy hiding all the contradictions."

"And what relative truth did your father believe?"

"Politics, you mean?"

"Yes, for example, politics."

"He believed in the things that now, suddenly, everybody believes in. He believed in social justice and democracy. He didn't let conventional wisdom persuade him that there can't be one without the other. No, he thought they were values that in a certain sense were antithetical and needed to be brought together as best one could. He was leery of great utopias. He believed in the gradual way, in the humble daily search for the lesser evil. Above all, he was democratic and at the same time a leftist. If he were English, he would have been proud to be a labourist. In Italy, as you know, the democratic left, blackmailed by the Catholics and brutalized by the communists, had come on bad times. So he voted for the Social Democrats, but without much enthusiasm, poor man."

"And you? Do you believe in the same things?"

"I think so. But just today I was asking myself what my life would have been like, in general, if I were left-handed. And my opinions as well, do you see . . ."

"Left-handed?"

"Yes, as I told you I recently discovered that I was probably born left-handed. I think I've already mentioned it. You yourself noticed I was handling the lobster cracker in reverse. It happens with all new movements. The ones I have to do instinctively, because no one ever taught me how to do them. I use my hands in reverse, awkwardly. As if one hand were the hand to use naturally, but is untrained, and vice versa. As if one had the knowledge but not the instinct, and the other the instinct but not the knowledge."

"Weird. And so?"

"The frontal lobes, you know . . . I don't know much about them except what I read in popular science articles. I think the right lobe controls a certain aspect of a person's life and the left lobe another—don't ask me exactly which side controls talent, or compassion, or courage, or rationality— that's not the point. Let's take someone destined to develop certain gifts more than others and turn him around. What happens? Will he continue to be the same or become some- one else? Will he follow his natural destiny or take a different route? And, more importantly, does natural destiny really exist? Is there a nucleus in each of us that's what it is and can't be anything else, or does everything—from our feelings to our deepest convictions to our moral sense—get dumped on us by a whim of chance, like trash into a garbage can? We consider our identity as a compact unit, but . . ." I paused for a second, then I went on. "You know, I suppose, what a dicotyledonous plant is?"

"Vaguely," he said, without conviction. The professor seemed to share the scant command of elementary scientific notions that all Italian intellectuals have.

"A dicotyledon, for example, has a seed divided in two halves. The baby plant, as soon as it sprouts, bears two identical little leaves. Let's say that human identity is like a dicotyledonous plant. However, one of the little leaves dominates; the other, though dominated, is present, like in an invisible mirror . . ."

"The subconscious ?"

"No, for God's sake! That's our dark side. I'm thinking of a secret twin that was not allowed to assert itself. Like the Iron Mask, remember?"

He blinked. I thought he, too, had been drinking too much .

"You know," I said, "on the plane I read an essay by one of your colleagues, not the worst among Italian philosophers; the opposite, I'd say. The title of it was "Praise of Intolerance." I think it was in the *Corriere*. A string of arguments that couldn't have repelled me more, intellectually or morally. But who can say? If my mother had allowed me to be left-handed, would I have agreed with them instead?

I realized I was babbling. The professor cracked a lobster claw and picked out twelve centimeters of meat whole. Then he surprised me with an appropriate remark, and I realized he was getting closer to what I was trying to say.

"This," he said, "could be a point supporting the parallax theory your father explained to you so simply and effectively. In a certain sense we might consider any ideological adversary as the incarnation of what we might have been if the least quirk of fate had forced us to develop in another way, so to speak. Doesn't that strike you as being a powerful argument in favor of tolerance? I look at my brother, my neighbor, my enemy, or even at the philosopher you mentioned, and every one of them is none other than myself in different circumstances. An imperceptible variance at the start, which in the course of time widens into a sea of differences."

"Yes, I know. In fact I'm considering it as a fantastic shortcut to apply to my work with the Machine. In the end the effect is always the same: to undermine this damned identity by forcing all the alternative hypotheses to come out of the shadows . . ." I sighed. "A great argument in favor of tolerance, but not a way of thinking that helps one make choices. It's as if everything were equally right, or equally wrong. It wouldn't be worthwhile to make any choices, just keep bumbling ahead."

"Let's get back to the subject," he pleaded. I had obviously been trying his patience. "You received your degree in Italy, from the University of Pisa, and then?"

"Then I got married. At the same time I volunteered as an assistant in the English Department."

I was beginning to get the hang of how to eat the lobster, just as a challenge, because I didn't like it much. Not even the rice was very good, overspiced by too many different herbs that got lost in a single heavy, indistinct flavor. My mother always used one at a time, at the most two complementary ones.

"They lasted two years, my marriage and the assistantship. I said bye-bye to both when it was clear there wasn't any future in either of them."

"I don't want to ask questions about your marriage, naturally, but I would like to know what made you think there wasn't any future for you at the university."

"To begin with, I wasn't a typical student. I went to classes when I could, I didn't participate in student life at all, I didn't go for a pizza with the others, or join sit-ins, or throw rotten tomatoes at the faculty. I didn't belong to any activist group. I didn't know anybody, and those were the years when the order of the day was to stick together, be part of a big group." I sighed and went on: "I was cooking meals for one of Italy's great gourmets and once a week I'd put together a memorable dinner for thirty or forty people. That would leave me time to study, which I was good at, but certainly not time to socialize."

"I understand."

I wonder if he really understood. "I was unmatched, like a single sock. I didn't have friends high up, I was a farmer's daughter, I was working as a cook. I didn't belong to any of the powerful ideological families: although born Catholic, I was not a believer, and I was a leftist liberal with a great aversion to Communism."

I must have gone on talking for quite a while. At ten o'clock, the professor took me home in his silver limousine.

5

I turned on the TV while I was undressing. Oh, my God!

A girl, about six or seven years old, wearing pink pajamas sprinkled with white teddy bears. Sitting on her bed. She didn't have any hair or eyebrows.

"When the doctor said I had cancer and was going to die, I didn't believe it," she said.

Her mother stood next to her, caressing her hand and smiling. "All her friends have promised to come see her for Christmas."

A voice off-camera. "What would you like for Christmas, Jennifer?"

The child smiled, too. "I'd like an autographed picture of Take That. And a kitten."

"I talked to Santa Claus just this morning," answered the off-camera voice, "and he said that's exactly what he's going to bring you." The child's smile broadened and her mother nodded.

I turned off the set, a knot in my throat. Is it really true that in this extraordinary country you've found a way to accept the idea of death? Did the child know what she was saying, or is there a secret procedure around here, an injection the doctor gives the gravely ill patient before explaining he's going to die? A shot of stoicism that turns the meaning of the word "death" around? Perhaps the doctor takes the patient into his office, pulls out his charts, studies the lab tests and—depending on the results—pushes a button under his desk. The nurse runs in with the needle and zap. Thirty seconds for the shot to take effect, and then: "I'm so sorry, sir," the doctor says in a very comforting but detached voice, "to have to tell you you've got two weeks, two months, two years to live. Don't take it hard, be happy. Death, after all, is quite natural. Of all the facts of life, death is the most certain, the simplest, the most democratic."

Is that what happens here? There must be a trick that gives you so much courage. Otherwise how could you be so different from us? How do you explain why Italian men and women—strong, aggressive, used to driving fast, smoking, living life as a continuous gamble—are incapable of facing death with the same grit a child in teddy bear pajamas has? There must be a trick!

I'm kidding. I know it's not like that. No tricks, no brainwashing, no drugs. Just more stoicism, perhaps less selfishness. Am I dying? All right. The important thing is not to leave anything hanging, to make sure the wife and kids are taken care of. And to live as well as possible in the time you have left. You decide to paint. You take a trip somewhere you've never been to but where you've always wanted to go— to that bend in the river where your grandfather used to take you fishing. To us, a reaction like that stinks to high heaven of being unreal. An edifying Lifetime TV movie. But it is true.

Death is real and you have to face it. To get used to it.

The wind came up and I had to close the windows. I drank a glass of mineral water and brushed my teeth. My thoughts drifted from one of our taboos to one of yours. I went back to something that sooner or later strikes us non-Anglo-Saxons visiting your country. You—I said to myself—so courageous, you who call death, cancer, AIDS, alcoholism by its name; you who don't hide from yourselves or from others any of the horrors that we go on denying right to the moment they do us in, you, ladies and gentlemen, don't install bidets in your bathrooms because you don't dare to officially recognize the existence of genitalia. It's an old story. Death, yes; private parts, no. God forbid. What an infinitely diametrical difference between you and us! Sure, you take showers in the morning, just as we do. But the rest of the day? You who make life so comfortable prefer to do real contortions when you have to wash down there rather than admit to the plumber that you also exist south of the beltline.

And yet, you're the ones who invented ramps and kneeling buses for those who can't manage stairs. You rightly remove physical obstacles. But what if anyone wants to wash where it's most needed more than once a day? Why don't you invent a sink that kneels down politely, like buses do, while keeping the austere name and look of a sink?

When I touched the power button to turn on the Machine, it was past midnight.

Wednesday: Salmon en Papier

I

As you know I have no classes on Wednesdays. The Machine was programmed according to my weekly schedule and tuned into my sleep one hour later than usual with the usual formula: "You're Italian but you live in New York. You're forty-two years old. This is my voice: yours. Tell our dream." When I was through, it brought me back to full consciousness with the appropriate phrase: "Your coffee will be ready in a couple of minutes. Take it easy today. Enjoy your day off."

The sun was high when I listened to my dream.

It's me and my husband . . . my ex-husband, Cesare. Everything is exactly as it had been in reality: the two of us living the perfect idyll in everyone's eyes, including our own. We're always alone together, our little house is our world. We never go anywhere. We hate mass tourism as much as arty vacations. We loathe consumerism, including the intellectual kind. We feel much superior to everyone else. Then an opportunity comes along, a sort of diplomatic mission, to take a free trip to an exotic country. Cesare explains to me that it's different from the usual trips with the herd; and besides, since it's free, we're not responsible. It's not as if we had chosen it. We set off with a very condescending attitude, ready to comment on the pointless vulgarity of it all. Our destination is a place by the sea, a green and white landscape: white cliffs, green fields, bushes. The water an emerald green. Poking along as if we were making a great sacrifice for someone who doesn't deserve it, we decide to have a picnic, just the two of us without the rest of the group. We soon come on an inlet littered with tin cans and trash floating in the crevices of the shoals. There's a large seashell caught among the rocks at the water's edge shaped like a toothy grin, or perhaps a tooth-lined vagina. The shell stinks of decay. We don't go swimming. Cesare starts throwing our empty cans and waste paper into the water; what difference does it make, he says, it's all disgusting any-way . . . I want to stop him but I can't because I have only one free hand. I hang on to the rocks with the other to stop from falling into the shell.

I sat up and had breakfast while listening to the dream the Machine had recorded. It was far from having any connection to the dream of the night before. But it didn't matter anymore. I had to start accepting the individual shadows of myself I was photographing night after night, without trying to justify them by piling them on one another in an absurd quest for substance. Indeed, who decides the minimal size of truth? Is the feather of a hummingbird less real than Mount Aconcagua?

Besides, I sensed that the image of myself that needed to be discovered was the left-handed one, to be placed next to the other, like the second little dicotyledonous leaf. From that moment on the dream—each dream in itself—would serve the amazing function of multiplying both of them, constituting two mirrored wholes, each containing a greater number of Martinas.

I had been clinging to the rock with my left hand. I couldn't prevent Cesare from throwing our garbage into the sea. Nor could I imitate him and get rid of unwanted ballast. What if I had been holding on with the other hand? It would have been the same. A single hand—left or right—wouldn't have been enough either to go along with my husband or to stand in his way. The point of it wasn't hands, but feet, and both counting equally. A solid base. A little safe ledge on which I could stand firmly with no risk of falling into the shell's horrible tooth-lined maw. That's the only way I could have been free to choose what to do.

A stupid dream. It faded from my memory, leaving behind a bad taste and embarrassment (envy?) over Cesare's behavior.

*   *   *

While I played bridge by myself, sitting up against the cushions my mother had embroidered for me before she became ill, I could see the barges slipping silently along the East River.

As happens whenever I see Cesare in my dreams, I was asking myself what on earth led me to marry him.

This is something that doesn't concern you, and I certainly shouldn't tell you about it. Yet how many of you suffer from feeling locked into an orbit far from the center of a real life, and, driven by an unbearable loneliness, are preparing to make choices as senseless as mine?

But would it be of any use to you if I told you my story? I doubt it.

In any case, whether I decide to tell it to you or not, things were tough for me at college.

Fear arose in me the very day Costantino left. You can't imagine the sweetness of those afternoons I spent with him on the Poggio di Mezzo. He would lay beside me and caress me for hours on end. There were tenderness and passion in his hands that I've never found since. Every part of my body was precious to him and became precious to me because of his touch.

For a reason I can't explain myself, it never occurred to either of us that our renunciation of complete love was a senseless sacrifice. For whom? I was the one who said no the first time. The words I spoke were obviously my mother's, my grandmother's, my great grandmother's, and the whole line of female forebears from Lucania with all their ancestral taboos.

"I'll do nothing you don't want," Costantino had said, and from that moment even our absurd renunciation became part of the bitter sweetness of our feelings for each other. But looking back on it, what foolishness.

One day he went away and left behind a vacuum. And the emptiness was awful, worse than anything. In a certain sense I had almost forgotten the pain of being separated from him, gripped as I was by the thought of loneliness. Loneliness had become a thing in itself. It no longer bore Costantino's image. It had a terrifying mask of its own. It seemed like a monster I could never defeat.

Essentially I convinced myself I'd never meet a man I could love. At the university the sense of isolation became an obsession. I would walk through the courtyard of the Sapienza and it seemed as if I were transparent.

From the very first day at the University of Pisa, I felt horribly certain that there wasn't anyone, not even among the freshmen, who didn't belong to a small group of at least five or six former classmates from the same prep school. They arrived in small bands, on the trains that picked up students from nearby cities. When we went into class they'd sit elbow to elbow on the benches, then they'd go out together to the pizzeria on the Lungarno. If one of them looked away from his own group as they chattered on and glanced around, he certainly wasn't looking toward a melancholic loner, but in the direction of other equally loud, self-assured groups who seemed to be in the know from the very first day. And at times two groups would band together, forming a larger and stronger one.

From the very first day they all knew the names of the university porters and classroom assignments, innately, one would think. I'd get lost wandering around the halls instead, always with an eye on my watch, fearful of wasting time. While the others went to the pizzeria, I'd run to the market with Dr Paoletti's shopping list.

Then I met Cesare. He was an assistant in the Philosophy Department, he, too, in his own way transparent. That was the reason, perhaps, that I hadn't paid him the least attention until I had occasion to ask for his signature on an exam schedule. Now I wondered how many other ghosts—like him, like me—haunted the courtyards of the Sapienza. And I ask myself if left-handed Martina would still have been one of them. If that was the case, would she at least have had the small comfort of being able to identify the other fellow loners around her? I ask myself if I had lived as a left-handed person, as I was supposed to be, would I have walked differently, thought, talked, listened differently?

Whatever. Cesare came out of the library and walked

to the street with me. He asked me if I'd eaten and invited me to share a pizza. That's how it began. I clung to him like a shipwrecked person to driftwood. And he? I don't know. Maybe it was the same for him too. He had just transferred and didn't know anyone.

After all, something could have happened between us, but it didn't. We got married, true, and tried to love each other. It was tough work. We continually reassured one another that everything was perfect, that our mutual intellectual understanding was unique. We were cloyingly kind to one another.

Nothing came out of it. Not even children. We didn't want any. We kept postponing from month to month . . . Just as well. It began without love and ended without crises. What I'm trying to say is my marriage, as a romantic episode, doesn't matter. Not as love, not as sex, not as anything. At times during those two years, and especially afterwards when I would meet other men, I used to think that it had been too perfect with Costantino, and nothing would ever work if I tried to compare it to what I had experienced with him. Then it became so clear that I even stopped thinking about it.

2

I stayed in bed till late.

As you know, I'd often go to my office even when I didn't have a class. I'd meet with some of you, I'd go to the library, read the papers, leaf through some books. I used to do research, but not anymore: there wasn't any literature about my work with the Machine.

This absence aroused different feelings in me, depending on the moment. At times it all seemed crazy, ridiculous. How is it possible that the same thought never occurred to anyone else, a voice said to me, a voice I tried not to hear. If all this had the slightest basis, it said to me, you really believe no one would have thought of it already? At times, however, I was quite certain that there was something to it, to my idea, even if I didn't know what. As if I had entered a dark room and brushed with my outstretched hands some object whose form and dimensions I could not make out. But there it was, right next to me.

I looked at the books on the library shelves—a great part of mankind's knowledge lined up on those walls. "Well," I said to myself, "until now nobody has added what I am about to take out of my hat. I will be the one to do it."

* * *

I followed the Machine's advice and took it easy. I got to the health club long after Jerry Keleti had left. I exercised for half an hour on Abdo-Trim and twenty minutes on Butt-Up, then went back to my apartment. I washed the floors with double concentrated Pine Fresh, I vacuumed the carpets and under every piece of furniture.

I decided to skip lunch. I gathered my laundry to take to the basement. It was two o'clock, a dead time in the Turtle Bay Tower laundry room. All the machines were free, the whole basement deserted. I poured a capful of Whisk, loaded the machine, put in five quarters, and went back up to my apartment to take a shower.

That's my special American game: everything has to be done at superhuman speed without a moment lost. In the time it takes the washer to go through its paces, I will do something else: the shopping, a shower, light gardening. Then I rush back downstairs with the recyclables, put the wash into the dryer, go to the other end of the basement and sort the bottles, cans and papers as the law requires. On my way back I stop at the bulletin board where the tenants tack their messages: that's how I bought my authentic colonial oak dining table when Sharon and Bill, from 12L decided to get rid of it to make way for a signed and dated *Saarinen*. I read the messages, make notes if necessary. At this point the dryer will have run through its twenty-minute cycle; so I return to my clean, dry laundry and fold it on the big table next to the machines. I go back up to the thirty-second floor, touch up some things with the iron, put everything away and I'm done. Forty-eight minutes is my record.

I get a strange, deep satisfaction from this ritual. And it's not even sufficient to call it satisfaction. It's something more. It's a sense of completeness, of profound coherence with the episode I'm living. It never occurs to me to say, "Martina is going down to the basement with her dirty sheets, she's counting her quarters, pouring the detergent . . . " I imagine many people experience this blissful completeness every day of their lives. But obviously I have to pay the price of the fascinating hypothesis I am working at. I am like a mouse gnawing at its trap. In my mind I am already out of it. For me, most of the time, being inside things that are happening is a much more precarious matter. They seem like events that don't concern me at all. Events I get into uninvited like a gate crasher at a party But I and my laundry are two nuts in a shell.

My mother must have guessed it, because she seemed more delighted by this American marvel than by any other. She'd do the totals, figuring out how much the whole procedure took me in terms of money and time. She told her friends about it, cheating a little. "It takes my American daughter a half hour to wash, dry and put away the laundry. With what it costs us to buy a washer she can do a thousand washes. And she doesn't have to hang the wash on a clothesline and then wait one or two days . . . if it doesn't rain, that is." I remember her voice so full of pride.

I went back downstairs, transferred the wash to the dryer, and took my load of paper, glass, plastic containers, and tin cans to the other end of the basement where the recycling bins are kept. It's like hell down there: hot, dark, drowned in the noise of the machinery that serves the vital functions of the building.

I didn't notice the sound, at first, mixed in as it was with all the noises. Then during a second's pause in the roar of the boilers I could hear it. It seemed like a moan.

Finding where it came from was not easy, because it was immediately reabsorbed in the general din. I put my garbage bag down and looked behind all the bins: two for bottles, two for newspapers, two for cans.

Then I began taking the lids off and looking inside: it was in the one for newspapers, sitting on the Arts and Leisure section of the Sunday Times, near a saucer that must have contained milk it had spilled or drunk. It was a puppy with long black fur, chubby and apparently healthy.

I left my laundry behind for a minute and took the puppy to the doorman.

"Somebody lost him in the basement," I said.

"Lost?"

"Abandoned. I found him in the newspaper bin."

I put the puppy down on Mr. Serrano's control panel. "I'll leave him to you," I said. "You'll have to give him back to whoever—let's say, lost him. Or find him a new home."

I thanked heaven to myself that he was there and not Mr. O'Mara or one of the two new doormen I don't know too well yet. Mr. Serrano is generally very considerate, even gallant. We have a tacit affection for each other. When he sees me dressed up, or in my evening clothes, he smiles at me in a special way to let me know my effort at looking my best—at least in his eyes—hasn't been wasted.

Actually he was very hard to convince. I had to give him twenty dollars and sign an agreement that I would take back the dog if he couldn't find him a family in the course of the day.

I went back down to the basement and pinned a notice on the cork board: "Cute black puppy needs a family." I put my name, apartment and phone numbers on it. I finished doing the laundry, went back to the apartment, remade my bed with the clean sheets, put the rest of my things in drawers and went out. I did the last tasks in a hurry because I had been struck by an idea.

3

I walked north to Fifty-third, then west for ten blocks. Oh, New York, New York.

The sky at the end of every street was an incredible electric blue. The wind blew from the east, stripping the trees of their leaves, some still green, whirling them toward the Hudson along with discarded Pepsi cans. In a few minutes, driven by the draft, I was at the corner of Ninth Avenue where my old apartment building once stood.

It had been rebuilt from the ground up, five or six times higher than before. It even had a name now, The Somerset House. There was a doorman, and the super was new. My nose was red, my eyes watering from the wind. Neither knew anything about Mrs. Schelucci. "When I came to America eighteen years ago, she was already living out of town," I said, "but since she was the one who found me an apartment in the tenement that used to be here, she obviously was familiar with the neighborhood."

I didn't expect them to understand the syllogism that was so un-American, but I knew that in Mrs. Schelucci's case it was right. A home for me had to be in an area that made her feel confident and comfortable. She would have found it by knocking at a neighbor's door, by talking to a friend. And before choosing an apartment, she would have checked the closets, the appliances. She never would have gone to a rental agency.

"When was this?" the doorman asked.

"Eighteen years ago, as I said. Almost nineteen."

"What? We just moved here from San Juan last Christmas."

Nineteen years is a long time in America . . . people change cities, change jobs, forget. And then they die, like everywhere else.

I went out into the street. In the four years since I left the old neighborhood it had been cleaned up even more. There was a new supermarket, restaurants I didn't remember, a new tarot reader, a new "Tan and Nails" like the thousands of identical places throughout the city. Other stores hadn't changed since they had opened while I was living there. The salad bar on the corner was the only place that I remembered from when I came from Italy that hadn't changed at all.

When I walked in, the only customer was leaving with a take-out and a cardboard container of coffee. Mrs. Paniotis was still at the cash register and she remembered me.

"Schelucci?" she shook her head, "I don't recall. How long ago was that?"

"Oh, ages. When I came from Italy they'd already gone."

She shrugged her shoulders. "Many years ago . . . Here they forget fast."

"Wait . . ." She was right but I didn't want to give up. "The memory of us Europeans," I said, " is something different. We look back to so many centuries." That was a silly thing to say. We can forget as easily as Americans. It's only that things back home last longer. We don't run the risk of forgetting because they're always there, century after century. It was a silly shot, but it worked.

Mrs. Paniotis smiled. "As for us Greeks, well, we go back thousands of years." She made a gesture of dismissal. "But here it's all plastic, and before plastic there wasn't anything. What would they use the memory for?"

She leaned over the counter. "What did you say her name was?"

"Schelucci, Marta Schelucci. You see, she found me an apartment in this neighborhood . . . It wouldn't have been like her to go through an agency. I'm convinced she was very familiar with this area, probably because she had lived here for a long time. She had a son, Costantino."

Mrs. Paniotis's face lit up. "Now I remember." She dribbled few drops of Clorox on a sponge and started wiping at the counter. "At first, when I heard her calling her son, I thought they were Greek too. The name is very common in our country. So we talked and she told me she was Italian. Of course, Schelucci. I remember now. She lived in one of the tenements around here."

"The one I lived in? The building they tore down to put up Somerset House?"

"Yes, I think so. But I'm not sure. I only knew her slightly. The seamstress who has that shop across the street was a friend of hers. She's Italian, too. Right there, across the street, on the second floor."

I was hungry. I had her make me a Greek salad and I ate it at the Formica counter, perched on a naugahyde-covered stool. As I left her, Mrs. Paniotis saluted me with five words in Italian :

"Ciao." Then, winking with an air of complicity: "*Una razza, una faccia.*"

I went across the street. The dressmaker's name was Guerriero. In her window she had a mannequin with half a paper jacket pinned to it. A sign read "Same Day Alterations."

"Marta Schelucci, sure I remember her," the dressmaker said in Italian. "She came to America the same year we did. Her husband was a big man. He was a construction worker, fell off the scaffolding, dead on the spot. Then there was Costantino, good-looking boy, quick. She rented an apartment in a building near here . . . it's gone now.

I interrupted her. "Not where Somerset House is now?"

"That's right. She was a very enterprising woman. She didn't speak English, she never learned to, but she managed all the same. She started by renting a spare room. Then she rented a bigger apartment and turned it into a boarding house. Her lodgers were mostly bachelors. Many Italians, obviously, but also others, of every kind. Singers in the Metropolitan Chorus, Julliard students. And girls—white, black—all colors. She cooked for them, did the laundry, ironed. She knew how to get on. She must have made money because she owned the building after a few years, the whole thing from top to bottom. When her husband died, she bought another one with the money from his insurance. Then another, and another. At the end, she almost owned the whole block. She sent her son to college, the best, very expensive. While she lived in this neighborhood, she never put on airs, despite her success. Then she sold everything, moved away, and never set foot here again. One fine day she says goodbye to her old friends and disappears. I don't even know where she moved to."

Mrs. Guerriero had learned little English and forgotten a great deal of Italian. She was locked into a hundred-word vocabulary held together by uncertain syntax. I thanked her, kissed her on both cheeks and went back to the high-rise that had gone up on the site of my old building.

"Can you tell me who owns this building?" I asked the doorman, and he gave me a business card that read "The White Eagle Group." It was the same company that owned the building I lived in on the East side. I should have guessed, considering that it was they who had offered me the apartment at Turtle Bay Tower.

I knew where their office was on West Fifty-seventh.

Things had come full circle, but it still wasn't going to be any easier. In this city where everything changes at an incredible rate, I had to find someone at the office who knew the present address of a farm woman from Lucania from whom the company had bought, twenty years ago, an old tenement that wasn't there anymore.

I did my shopping in the old neighborhood, taking more time than I had planned. I stopped by to say hello to Harvey Moss in his tiny bookstore. He had a first edition of *The Spoils of Poynton* put aside that he charged me only forty-five dollars for.

When I got on the bus I realized I was going to be late for my appointment with Professor Cerignola. I sat in one of the single seats on the left side of the bus and prayed for a fast bus ride

It wasn't. Few of the people boarding the bus had a card or a token, and we had to wait while they dug around for their dimes and quarters to put into the slot. At Forty-second Street, the bus had to kneel for a young man with a leg in a cast. Two blocks before my stop another delay while the driver let down the rear door for a woman in a wheelchair. I conformed to the strict American code: I didn't sigh, I didn't raise my eyes to heaven, I didn't keep looking at my watch. I figured I was going to be fifteen minutes late.

*   *   *

Mr. Serrano was off by the time I got home. Mr. O'Mara was on duty and in a very bad mood. The puppy was under his desk.

"You can't leave the dog here," he said.

"No one's been by to claim him?"

"Certainly not; in this building we've got dogs that are worth three, four thousand dollars. No mutts around here."

"But still, someone must have put him in the basement. One of these grand people with dogs worth three to four thousand dollars."

"You brought the dog here, it's your problem."

I tried smiling. "I'm running very late tonight. Couldn't you hold on to him till tomorrow and see if someone wouldn't be willing to adopt him?"

"That's out of the question." He bent over, picked up the puppy from under the desk, and thrust him into my arms. "Take it to a vet and have it put down."

I looked at my watch. I only had a few minutes to take a shower and change before Professor Cerignola would arrive.

In the elevator the dog threw up on my jacket.

I had to rinse off the stain before it dried, make a bed for the dog, put water in a bowl and half a thawed hamburger in another. I listened to a couple of messages on the answering machine, but no one wanted the dog.

When the doorman rang on the intercom to let me know Mr. Cerignola was waiting in the lobby, I was still naked and my hair was still wet. I did what I could to it with the hair dryer, slipped into a simple black sheath, locked the dog in the bathroom with his bed and bowls, grabbed my purse, a coral necklace, my pink Versace jacket, and dashed to the elevator. On the way down I finished dressing and at six-thirty, only a half hour late, I was standing at the door of Sebastiano Cerignola's limousine.

4

He kissed my hand and ushered me into the car. The limo's interior was the size of my kitchen. He gave the driver the address of a small French restaurant on Jane Street in the Village. He had a pile of about eight or ten Italian newspapers on his lap. During the drive he kept thrusting one after the other at me and pointing to some of the headlines. "You see," he said.

I didn't see. They were the same old headlines, and I said so.

"That's the point. We . . ." He said "we" with some embarrassment. ". . . we have gained, in a certain sense, a great deal of power, recently, but the press still treats us with the same condescension as four or five years ago, when our support in the country still hadn't been taken into account."

Now I finally began to understand who had sent Professor Cerignola to talk to me. I could imagine him walking along on the grounds of some exclusive resort with a group of powerful politicians. I could even hear their telegenic voices: "Go to New York and talk to Martina Satriano," they were saying. What I couldn't figure out was what they wanted from me.

He signaled the driver to pull over at the corner of

West Fourth. We got out and walked two blocks under the golden gingko trees. The street was full of couples—of the same or different sex. It was like strolling in a Paris much more Parisian than Paris, France. This one was more like the Paris in American songs: everybody was uniformly unconventional. Everybody seemed to be in love, arty. I wondered whether their outfits should be defined as chic poor or throwaway expensive. We sat at a sidewalk table, and it was we who looked eccentric, I in my Versace suit and he in his impeccably tailored pinstripe that seemed to have been cut by a laser beam.

"No aperitif for me," I said. We ordered *salmon en papier*, tossed salad, and a *tarte Tatin*.

"The press is by nature 'anti,'" I said. "I could list several examples."

"I could, too. They know they'll sell more copies taking very little risk. But that's not what I wanted to talk about."

A young man sitting on the steps of the house across the street began playing his guitar. His head was shaved and he had a light beard, which combined with his ash-gray T-shirt and his washed-out black jacket, made his pale skin look paler.

"About what then?"

"About the fact that we have the votes but not the cultural prestige. Maybe I should call it aesthetic and cultural prestige. We don't have intellectual backing and what's more we're not chic, we're not snobs, we're not witty, we're not good-looking. We're the ideal targets of ridicule. We've set ourselves up as the victims of a particular kind of political attack. The kind that starts with the ploy of *mettre les rieurs de son coté*, as the French say."

It was an expression I'd never heard. "It's an expression I've never really understood," I said.

"It means bringing over to your side those who like to amuse themselves at someone else's expense. The reader with a sneer always handy, the typical reader, I'd say. From the time of the Circus Maximus, cruelty in all its aspects has been the favorite form of entertainment, as you well know."

On a summer's night two years before, I had made love among the ruins of the Circus Maximus. This episode I might censor out of the story, if I decide to turn it in to a lesson for you. Would you understand why I made love to a total stranger? I doubt it. I haven't even been able to explain it to myself. He was an Australian who was seated next to me on the New York–Rome flight. At Leonardo da Vinci they told us domestic flights were cancelled because of a strike, so we had to stay overnight. I took him on a tour around the city, then we went to a little restaurant in Piazza della Consolazione.

After dinner we strolled for a while, and found ourselves in a little dark street that ended at the Circus Maximus.

There was nothing cruel about the games we played in

the gladiators' arena. The night air was soft. We both had our clothes off. The broken outline of the Baths of Caracalla stood against the western horizon. We could sense more than hear the roar of the city all around us. But it seemed as if the sounds closer to us—the crickets in the grass, a nightingale in the blackberry bushes—were protecting us with a wall of music. The sky was full of stars, the grass smelled sweet, Patrick's voice was soothing.

The salmon was superb. I poked about the wrapping with my fork to identify the julienne greens and herbs the salmon steak was lying on. Zucchini, celeriac, I couldn't tell what the third was. Then dill and mint.

Mint like the kind that grew among the stones of Circus Maximus and permeated the air around us. Patrick and I parted without exchanging addresses: a perfect night minus the risk of later disappointments.

"I've never had such a good toyme in my loyfe," he noted as we said goodbye. I don't know what I replied in my Italian accent. You see, I don't remember how many years it is, since events I live through are not converted into memories. What happened in the Circus Maximus is not a memory. Only the smell of mint and a name—Patrick—which, thinking about again, I am not even sure of. Maybe his name was Andrew.

* * *

"That's why we need all of you," the professor said.

"All of whom?"

"All you intelligent, cultured, witty, good-looking, chic, cosmopolitan types who didn't find a place in the cultural center of the first republic."

It's too late now to worry anymore, the boy with the guitar was singing. Another young man was now sitting next to him: same beard, same hair, same defenseless thin neck sticking out of his black coat. Both wore the style, now prevailing among the gay community of this city, that assumes as an aesthetic pattern the look of so many friends with AIDS. Is this gesture of solidarity deliberate? Maybe it's just an instinct, a compassionate, caring instinct.

"Look, professor, I'm not chic. I wouldn't have had to leave Italy if I were. Furthermore, I deplore chic. It's the only value that's based on inequality. One can be healthy in a world of healthy people, beautiful in a world of beautiful people, intelligent in a world of intelligent people, even rich in a world of rich people, but one is chic exclusively by reason that others are not. Chic is nothing more than a measure of the distance between a lucky individual and common mortals."

I offered him a tasty morsel and he darted at it like a hungry trout. "To think," he cried, "the only part of the Italian left that enjoys a major following is shot through with chic. Intellectuals speaking with a French *R* and frequenting the salons, elegant ladies with upturned noses. People who would have taken the first plane to the United States, or even to Pinochet's Chile or Franco's Spain, if communism had really taken over in Italy."

"My ex-husband doesn't speak with a French *R*, but vacations at Capalbio. My sister Carmelina told me the other day."

"Then I guess he was successful. Even if, I believe, Capalbio is no longer the ultimate resort for the Italian left."

"Really? How sad for Cesare, poor man. He's only just achieved it. He saved for years to realize his ambition of owning a rustic cottage near his big shots. I imagine at that point it was too late to change the direction of his dreams. In any case he's got there, and that means he's successful, as you said."

A waitress who looked like Jeanne Moreau brought our tarte Tatin.

"It was long climb for Cesare. During the first year we were married he taught at Cagliari; he managed, but not brilliantly. Then I realized that while he was making a career for himself, certain events were disappearing from his memory. He was a great storyteller—some people thought he was boring, but I didn't. I liked listening to him. He was five years older than I—he'd studied in Milan at the Statale University. All during our engagement and the early part of our marriage—you know how husbands are when they keep recounting the same things over and over again—he'd tell me about his childhood, his family, and mostly about his university. They were stories meant to demonstrate something. Stories with a moral."

"Oh?"

"Yes. They all had a common denominator—a visceral repugnance toward Moscow that extended to those who, according to him, didn't distrust Moscow enough."

"I see."

"Episodes that contributed to giving shape not so much to his opinions as to the flesh and blood his opinions fed on. All grounded on physical intolerance, perhaps envy . . . there wasn't any love of democracy, of freedom . . . they weren't my father's open-minded convictions. There was nothing positive about them."

I realized I was blushing when I hastened to add: "Certainly there's no more severe and probably unjust a judge than a divorced wife."

The professor gestured for me to continue, as if to express his confidence in my fairness. I went on:

"The rational part of his opinions was not so different from mine . . . Not even I, you see, not even when I was eighteen, the age when one falls in love with utopias, ever wanted Italy to go communist. Only that he went further, adding a real hatred. It was a personal issue between him and what was then known simply as the Party, a seething anger that lived off of a whole storehouse of memories. He would tell me stories and it was as if, remembering them, he were recharging the batteries of his resentment. Like the story of the '68 generation teenager from the provinces—from Treviso, I think—who went to Milan to see the very center of the juvenile protest, to meet his idols. He wanted to make a good impression, so he spent his savings on a complete new outfit. New jacket, new pants, new shirt, new shoes, new tie. All shined up, nineteen years old, candid and enthusiastic as a puppy. When he went into the courtyard of the Statale the others saw him as too decked out, not really one of them . . . they took him for a fascist and killed him. Not beat up, professor, killed."

He seemed quite struck. "I hadn't heard about this."

"But, you see, it may not even be true. At a certain point, Cesare stopped talking about it, just as he had stopped talking about a lot of other things. Events he had come back to again and again during the early years seemed to have disappeared from his memory without leaving a trace. And if I asked what had happened to those stories, if I tried to make him remember, he'd slip away like an eel. I couldn't tell when he'd manipulated those stories to fit his purposes. Before, after . . . How could I know? As far as I knew those stories might never have been true, but then it didn't matter to me anymore. What had lost value and meaning weren't those stories, it was he, my husband."

"And so you got a divorce."

*　*　*

Across the street a young man darted by on the sidewalk, riding a homemade scooter. Two wheels like the ones in D'Agostino's carts, two boards, a lawnmower motor. He was wearing a yellow corduroy miniskirt, a green sweater, cowboy boots.

"Yes, after a while. I began to think about many things—the work, the patience . . . I thought, for instance, about my father's watch. It was an automatic . . . I don't think they make them anymore. It seemed like a great invention when I was small. They wound themselves when you moved your arm. It had been given to my father by his fellow workers on the Potenza-Foggia line when he was forced to retire. He dearly loved it. Because it was a memento of his friends, a link to the South, a professional recognition—and then the object itself. He was proud of its technical perfection. It seemed to him that he possessed in advance a piece of the great future that awaited mankind. A civilization that produced such a marvel, he thought, would know how—gradually—to secure the happiness of every man. He'd take me on his knee, wave his left arm close to my ear, and let me listen to the soft sound his Movado Kalendomatic made while it was rewinding.

"When he was run over by his tractor, he suffered for four days before dying, and during those four days—you can't imagine what sorry condition he was in—he put all his failing strength into keeping that watch going. His left forearm was one of the few parts of his body he could still control, and he'd pump it up and down for a few minutes every six hours.

"Mamma and I took turns watching over him at night, and when I was sitting by his bed in the dark, I could hear the soft whirring of his watch as it rewound itself. Then when my father died we forgot about the watch, and when we went to get it, it had stopped . . . stopped forever. It wouldn't react if we moved it, so we tried rewinding it the traditional way, but it was useless. Papa had pumped his arm up and down while he was dying, and we hadn't even taken the trouble to render him the final honor of keeping his Movado Kalendomatic alive."

I finished my *tarte Tatin* and laid my fork on the plate.

"I don't know. I don't know how this is connected with my marriage or with my divorce. The fact is that when Cesare began to make a name for himself at the university, the memory of my father, the story about the watch and so many other stories, and the memories of the family—my mother, the preserves, the dried tomatoes, the toil, the patience, the moral earnestness—all that, I thought, doesn't jibe with a man who has memory as adaptable as rubber."

Jill Clayburgh, escorted by a young man with a beard, came over, sat at the table next to ours and ordered a vichyssoise. We asked for two espressos.

"It didn't matter to me," I continued, "whether he had

manipulated the truth by telling me certain things first or by denying them afterward. I didn't care which. I was disgusted with him. I didn't have any friends my own age. I couldn't participate in the general enthusiasm for our generation, so reluctant to accept concrete personal responsibilities and so ready to replace them with a petulant, childish presumption, that taught everything to everyone without bearing the burden of anything." I laid my napkin next to my plate. I was tired and wanted to go to bed.

"In short," I concluded, "Cesare had disappointed me, I wasn't achieving anything in Italy, so I left both of them: him and Italy. It was a quick decision and I've never regretted it. I landed in a country that wasn't mine, I presented my credentials, I was listened to, evaluated, and hired. I didn't know anybody, I wasn't recommended by anyone. No one asked my political opinions. That's how it works here."

Cerignola took me home at eleven. It was more and more obvious that he wanted to offer me something precise, but he still hadn't told me what it was. And what bothered me most was not knowing what he would ask in return. He got out of the limousine and escorted me to the elevator. "We should have another evening together. There's a nice little place on Sixty-fifth. I'll be by to pick you up at the same time," he said.

He was going from one expensive restaurant to another, dashing about town in a silver limousine. Now that I was beginning to understand who was paying the bills, the purr of the departing Lincoln seemed softer than ever.

The puppy had unrolled the toilet paper and shredded it to bits, five centimeters of snow strewn over the bathroom floor. He was chewing on a piece. I took it out of his mouth. "Did you eat it? How much did you eat? You'll get a tummy ache." I had to clean up the bathroom before locking him into it again. I knew that the next day I'd probably have to have him put down, but I didn't want him to spend his last hours with an upset stomach. As I swept the floor, he went into the bedroom and lay down beside the bed with his head resting on his forepaws. He wagged his tail when I came back in and looked up at me. I carried him back to his own bed and set the Machine for six o'clock. Before going to bed, I went down to the basement to change my notice. The new one read: "Black puppy, cute and loving, needs a family."

No one was around. While I was waiting for the elevator, the lights suddenly dimmed for a few seconds then came back again. My heart fluttered as I remembered that an execution was scheduled that very night in a neighboring state. This enviably civil society was getting rid of an undesirable human being by roasting him in the electric chair, thus maintaining its high degree of perfection. And perhaps I had participated physically in this proper American method for dealing with human trash as I stood in a basement darkened by the instant surge of power an electric chair had required to dispatch its victim.

I got into the elevator with a sigh of relief. Maybe, I thought, the state I was thinking of didn't employ the electric chair anymore and had subscribed to the latest fashion of administering death by lethal injection. Paramedics gowned in white, right out of a TV soap-opera. I can imagine them as young, friendly, good American guys, their minds and hearts trained for helping, for understanding. They approach the prisoner strapped on the gurney. Do they smile? Possibly. Do they swab the skin with alcohol to disinfect it before the needle is inserted? It seems like a waste of money and of time, which is also money. But this society, as well as being civil, is rich.

For the most part, those who oppose capital punishment ask, "And what if the condemned man is innocent?" I answer: "But even if he is guilty?" Can a human being, in all conscience, be *disposed of? To dispose of* is such a neutral, virtuous act. There is no nastiness in it. It means to move something gently toward nonbeing, something that preferably should not be. No hard feelings. The way we get rid of garbage.

Or rather the way we used to. Now, damn it, we recycle everything. There, a few meters across the basement, is the door to the room where local laws compel us to separate into labeled bins our empty Progresso tomato and Pepsi cans (rinsed), plastic bottles, glass bottles (divided by color) and newspapers (bundled and neatly tied). From there, each item is dispatched to useful and dignified ends.

The whole procedure is expensive and demands co-operation from the citizens, but it's worth it, they say, and I'm sure it is, because I know that in my crowded and irre-sponsible country where they don't do enough about it, there will soon be a time when they'll be buried under a mountain of their own garbage.

But is it possible that you—so competent and civil—can't invent another sort of trash bin (not in my basement, if you don't mind) where the irreplaceable sparkle of life that is housed in a human being, no matter if a criminal human being, can be stored temporarily before being sent off to be recycled somehow? Isn't it a little too casual just to switch it off?

Thursday: Artichokes alla Giudia

I

I dipped the warm croissant into my coffee. My voice began speaking from the Machine.

> *I'm in a Volkswagen van with a group I don't know. Cesare is there, too, but he's sitting up front. Maybe he's driving, maybe he's sitting next to the driver. I'm in back, perched on my suitcase, in the corner diagonally opposite him. I'm facing the rear door watching the road unwind behind us through a small round window. At a curve, a motorcyclist following too closely seems distracted for a moment and knocks against our bumper. The van doesn't stop, and the cyclist gets very angry. Then he begins banging against us deliberately, risking injury to himself mainly, but the driver doesn't pay attention. Finally the repeated banging shakes the door loose and it swings open. The young man on the motorcycle throws something inside that looks like a Molotov cocktail and only then does the driver stop. I jump out and confront the cyclist: "You could*

have been killed—whatever possessed you to do something so stupid, and besides you were in the wrong and what the hell did you throw at us?"

Now I'm on the bike hanging on behind the cyclist, my arms wrapped around his tight, hard body. I like the feel of his strength and warmth. Maybe we've already spoken with our eyes when he was following us. Now the open door of the van seems to me to be a prison gate and the boy my liberator. I recklessly run away with him. My only problem is that when I jumped out of the van, my belt must have ripped off, along with some buttons from my shirt-dress. I'm clutching it closed like a robe so I won't be naked. The young man takes me to have a drink on a terrace high up. "If you really want to know this country, I'll be your guide," he says. "I can't," I answer, "I don't have my belt."

As we're leaving the bar he steals a napkin for me. I fold it diagonally and make a belt out of it. His teeth stick out a little as if a smile inside his mouth were pressing against them to get out. I feel a tenderness for him that melts my heart.

I'm crying as I give him a kiss. "I have to leave you now," I say. "My three little children are waiting for me." I run to the bus station, looking for a telephone, but I don't know who to phone, no one understands me, the police are armed to the teeth, the radios aren't receiving, the transmitters aren't transmitting, the telephones don't work. And I have a napkin on instead of a belt. The policemen around me look more and more like nurses, their weapons more and more like surgical instruments. I go into labor and finally give birth.

No sooner had I understood that my work should no longer be focused on pasting my separate dreams together, but rather on evaluating them one by one as hypothetical versions of my left-handed life, than came a dream that seemed to be the next chapter of the one I dreamed the previous night.

I skipped my bridge game. While I slipped into a robe, I thought, "I've never in my life owned anything like the shirt-dress buttoned from top to bottom I was wearing in my dream." I considered it an important point. The woman in the dream was me, but at the same time another woman, one of the infinite number of women I could have been. Only later that afternoon did I realize I had concentrated my attention on the most trivial difference, forgetting the tendency to run away with unknown young men on motorcycles, the three children who were waiting for me at home, and the final birthing on the floor at the bus station.

Was it the boy on the motorcycle who had given me a real child? Had I made up the other three; were they an excuse so that I could get away from him? Or were the real ones at home, forgotten, while I was running away in search of another country? And was this a right-handed or a left-handed dream?

*   *   *

I brushed my hair and went over to knock on Jerry Keleti's door. I knew that his really sacrosanct hours when he was not to be disturbed were the ones he dedicated to reading, to his VCR, to whiskey. At that moment he was working and seemed to enjoy the interruption.

"You have to help me locate somebody," I said.

"Sure. Sit down, have a coffee."

We went into his living room, the twin of mine, facing the East River. Just then the sun rose over the rooftops of Queens. Jerry turned off the light and we went to sit by the window with our mugs. "I need to find out something that concerns my childhood, and here in America there's a woman who might be able to help me, if she's still living."

He didn't ask for explanations. I was glad about that.

Jerry takes his dreams into reality and his reality into dreams in a continuous time span, which is neither day nor night but a sort of uninterrupted twilight. He's the most monolithic creature I know. He earns his living by ferrying words across from one language to another, but he doesn't have the split personality conventionally attributed to translators. He doesn't think half in French and half in English but in a supranational language without words, the language of Tolstoy, Stendhal, Howard Hawkes. His world is inhabited by friendly shadows that always agree with him. His opinions are like granite. About himself he says proudly "I am factious."

Encased in his armor of habits, opinions, inclinations, he is like a tiny and incredibly heavy mass, in which each element forever folds back into itself, constantly imploding, never exploding. I had talked to him only very little about the Machine. I knew I couldn't have got him to understand my intent to reveal the precariousness of the so-called "I" by setting next to it a nocturnal shadow that was taking on more solidity as the dreams started connecting to one another. Nor could I tell him that I was now trying to achieve the same end by reappropriating a hypothetical left-handed identity. It was not easy to ask a man like him—while we sipped our coffee and the sun was rising over Queens—to help me prove I was someone else.

"Where do we begin?" he asked.

"I have her given and family name and her last known address. And I know that the White Eagle Corporation bought a tenement building from her on the West Side. Then she moved to Long Island."

"When was that?"

"Twenty years ago, perhaps longer."

"That's a very long time. This isn't Europe. Things move faster here."

"I know. But if I could find someone at the White Eagle, someone who's been there a number of years . . . I've always paid the rent through my bank, so I don't know anyone there. Do you?"

"Well, I do know one of the secretaries . . . Rosalie, do you remember her? I went out with her a couple of times. She hasn't been there that long, but I believe her boss is the man who started the company."

"Call her, please."

He looked at his watch. "In a couple of hours. She got married. Right now she's in bed with her husband."

"Will you remember to do it?"

"Certainly."

"And . . . another thing. Wouldn't you like to have a dog?"

"Very much."

"Great . . . I have just what you need."

"Wait a minute. I would like one if I were rich, lived in the country, had an old and trusty housekeeper to care for it when I don't have the time . . . Otherwise do I look like the kind of guy who gets himself into complications? I'm selfish and don't want any commitments."

I asked him to walk me to my apartment. I opened the door to the bathroom and the puppy rushed out wagging his tail.

"Isn't he cute?"

"Yes indeed." Jerry leaned over to scratch him between the ears and the dog immediately rolled over, his soft belly trustingly exposed, his mouth gaping in an ecstatic smile, his carnation pink tongue hanging out.

"Where did he come from?"

"I found him in the trash, and I don't know what to do with him. I'd hate to have him put down."

"Poor little guy." Jerry straightened up and headed toward the door. "I'll call you at the office the minute I find out something."

He phoned at two that afternoon, while I was correcting papers. "His name's Kevin Shell. He's the president of the company, has an apartment on Central Park South. He's not married. He owns a minor league soccer team. He's a patron of Carnegie Hall. He works very hard. Except when he's away on business you can always find him in his office on West Fifty-seventh Street from nine in the morning till six at night. That is, if he'll see you."

I put the papers away and rushed out to catch the subway. His office was on the thirty-fourth floor. The receptionist's name was Aurora Massey, as one could read on the brass plate sitting on her desk. She must have been one of the customers of the city's "Tan and Nails," not for her tan—she was black—but for her nails, which were extravagantly long and painted in a turquoise and gold mosaic pattern. She gingerly pushed a blank form toward me with her fingertips. It had to be filled out with my name, address, telephone number, and my reason for wanting to see Mr. Shell. I couldn't very well say "to find out where Mrs. Schelucci is now." I printed PERSONAL MATTERS.

"We'll let you know," the receptionist said.

"When?"

"Later this afternoon."

When I got back I found the answer on my message machine. I was given a choice of three dates. I called back and made an appointment for the earliest one, the next day at noon.

2

I went down to the subway station and took the E train to the Fourteenth Street stop. From there I walked west for three blocks to the piers along the Hudson. I had never been in that part of the city, but I always wanted to find out if, as the map pinned to my kitchen door showed, a wide boulevard closed to cars ran along the river.

It wasn't really a boulevard, but two cement strips that together measured nearly eighty meters in width. The western side running along the river was reserved for bikers and skaters. The other strip was a sort of no-man's land dotted with a few trash barrels, some structures that must have been illegal—a trailer selling house plants, a stand selling hot dogs and coffee—and large, unidentifiable, and probably abandoned objects wrapped in black plastic.

The roadway disappeared in the distance. I figured you could walk, bicycle, or skate for several kilometers without running into traffic. Maybe even as far downtown as the World Trade Center and Battery Park.

The weather had changed the last few days. The air was clear and chilly. I took out the wool cap I have learned always to keep in my purse starting from the first of October. I pulled it down over my forehead and began walking south.

I had read in the paper that eight sea turtles left behind during their annual migration were found stranded half-frozen on the shore near Riverdale. A wildlife organization had taken them to the Oceanographic Institute for treatment. People were being asked to look out for other animals stranded on the shore. I walked along the Hudson, smooth as glass, but didn't spot any turtles. Some sea birds were diving underwater, oblivious of the cold, in search of fish among the pilings of the abandoned piers.

I recalled that from there just a while ago the *Rex*, the *Conte Grande*, the *Ile de France*, the *Queen Elizabeth* used to set sail.

Seeing those rotting wharves made a strange impression on me. Even the fences that separated them from the walkway and the warning signs were falling to pieces, ruin upon ruin from a time so recent and so irreparably lost.

I walked south as far as Pier 45, abandoned like the rest but still accessible. I headed toward the end of the pier. The sun was setting right in front of me, beyond the river, slowly disappearing between two red brick towers on the Jersey side. A red swath glistened on the water, and even the cement at my feet was turned to a fiery red.

Three or four off-leash dogs were sniffing at each other with great gusto. Their owners were gathered midway on the pier, sipping coffee from paper containers, swapping notes on canine behaviour. As I walked by, they greeted me and looked around to see which was my dog. I waved and continued on toward the very end of the pier. Looking to my left, I saw—for the first time in my life—the Statue of Liberty.

That's right, in twenty years I'd never been to pay my respects. A rather obvious trip, I told myself. And besides, it's an ugly statue.

To tell the truth, just the thought made me panic. I knew that if I had arrived in America two generations earlier, there would have been the anguish of the break from home, the fear of the unknown, the humiliation of Ellis Island, the leap into the hostile void of an unknown language. That towering woman with the upraised hand would have meant more of a threat than a welcome to me. A nasty attendant in a cruel insane asylum. A guard in a women's prison. You, Martina Satriano. Strip, let's see if you're healthy, clean, up to the standards of this country.

So I was seeing her for the first time from Pier 45, and I was seeing her from behind her back. If we can suppose she was guarding the city from her little island, then I had already sneaked across the lines. "You don't scare me anymore, Madame," I said. A ship was leaving the port, a small cruiser flying the Italian flag. Well, it could even have been Mexican, or Hungarian. But I don't think so. It all seemed to hang together, better than a comforting dream: the dusk, the statue, the ship. Even the dogs.

I thought if I decided to keep the puppy, I might move to an apartment in the West Village, between Bank and Christopher Streets. I could give up my morning bridge game, and I, too, could walk my dog on the pier before going to work. Like the other owners, I could hold my container of coffee, and my dog would have his ball to play with like the other dogs. I would have the usual plastic bag in my pocket, ready to obey the rule about cleaning up after your dog that was posted on signs every fifty meters. If I didn't do it better than the others, the statue would turn on me and accuse me: I saw you, you dirty wop. Yes, that's the way you all are.

3

While waiting for Professor Cerignola, I turned on the TV. Julia Child prepares a *tarte Tatin*. Julia Child, the honorary dean of American Cordon Bleus, for countless years TV's top star of haute cuisine. Mrs. Child, before starting, rambles on about apples: which ones are and which ones are not the best for the famous tart that the Tatin sisters created in Paris at the beginning of the century. She describes at least fifteen varieties and shows them to us, taking each out from the different baskets lined up on her counter. This one's quite good, this one's not; this is so-so, this never ever, please. She speaks in an accent that to my foreign ears sounds English: soft, almost wadded, as if a piece of one of her apples were stuck between palate and nose. I like that accent. Much more than yours, believe me. "I cayn't staynd this buck," as one of you said just yesterday. I agree, essentially. I, too, my dear, consider that book a bore. But that meowing!

Anyway, Mrs. Child's accent—aspirating whatever needs to be aspirated, opening whatever needs to be opened, and narrowing as little as possible—assures her audience that she has good luck with apples. She points to a basketful of the very, very best ones. Unfortunately they can only be found if you live in the country, in one particular region, and at only one time of the year.

Now she disappears and the commercials come on for three minutes. Then Julia is back and starts with the dough. She declares that she's only recently been converted to machines, after ages of doing everything entirely by hand. She puts flour, sugar, and whatever else is needed into a mixer, turns it on, and is immediately enveloped in a white cloud. Almost all the ingredients have been blown about, but the lady keeps her composure. "There's also this other type of mixer," she says, turning to a huge semi-industrial device on the counter, in which she drops the remaining spoonfuls she's managed to scrape out of the other mixing bowl.

The second food processor works better, and finally she unsticks a few shreds of dough from the blades. Julia rolls them into a ball, puts it into the fridge, and turns to the apples. "This," she says, "is going to be an upside-down pie. Therefore, you have to cut perfect crescents to form concentric circles. And of course, as I said," she repeats, "the variety of the apples is vital. They shouldn't cook down to mush. I'll teach you a trick," she adds. "Slice them ahead of time, sprinkle with sugar and lemon juice and put them in the fridge for a couple of hours. They will release a lot of liquid you can drain off, so you won't have a runny pie."

She takes her presliced apples from the fridge, drains them, arranges them in the pie tin in exact concentric circles, eliminating the slices that aren't perfect half-moons. Covers them with the dough. Puts the tin in the oven. Commercials.

Now she's back. It's time to take the creation from the

oven . . . Julia unmolds the *tarte*. "I'm not really sure it's perfect," she says.

She turns the product onto a plate: no, it is not perfect. It's a gray, runny mess . . . a lava flow. The apple slices have disintegrated. The whitish dough has slid to one side in a sorry heap.

"It sometimes happens," says Julia without letting herself be discouraged. "Now I'll show you how you can make up for the disaster." She affectionately taps the thing here and there with a spatula, trying to center it, but the attempt is useless, with everything flowing on every side. She is quite content nonetheless. "We've got it all under control now," she says. "We put the tart, as it is, under the broiler to brown it. Just a couple of minutes ought to do it."

While waiting, she proceeds unperturbed to enlighten the audience on one of the essential virtues of a great chef: to be able to turn accidents into perfection.

Then she takes the *tarte* out of the oven and brings it to the other side of the studio. It's a ritual in many of her shows: at the end she sits at her pretty dining table, with the embroidered table cloth, the lobelias in a vase, the right bottle of wine to go with the dish of the day. "Let's have a taste," she says.

The camera zooms in on the *tarte*, which in the meanwhile has spread out to the rim of the plate. Julia has a silver cake knife ready, but, driven by the instincts of a great cook, understands that this time it's not a suitable utensil. So she grabs a spoon, and eats her *tarte Tatin* as if it were a soup. "Not too bad," she clucks in her English accent. "But I don't know," she adds loyally, "what the Tatin sisters would have thought of it." Credits—French music—end of the show.

You see, this struck me, the envious Mediterranean, as model Anglo-Saxon behavior. Oh America, America!

Julia Child—although certainly annoyed—didn't allow herself to be upset by her flop. And she didn't try to escape her embarrassment by being funny. She didn't say, as an Italian TV star would have said, "Well, this is the fun of live TV."

Besides, it wasn't live. The program had been taped months, maybe years ago, that's the amazing thing. It could have been redone to perfection. Moreover, Mrs. Child could have played it safe by having a beautiful *tarte* ready in the wings to replace her pitiful *soupe Tatin* during the commercials. She could have had one delivered from the French restaurant where Professor Cerignola had taken me. Or she could have kept plastic pies, roasts, soufflés on hand in the TV studio to cover up disasters.

But in this country, normally, one isn't supposed to lie, not even on TV, not even when the subject is a mere apple pie. Some politicians sometimes lie, but—thank God—it still causes a big scandal, even after Nixon. At least that's what we foreigners think, and Julia Child had just confirmed it.

And I? I was moved by the frankness of this old American lady, with her accent, her tablecloth, her lobelias in the vase. That, you see, was the kind of situation I would never have seen on Italian TV. In a way it was the very reason I was living in America. I don't exaggerate: I was moved.

But I am Italian, after all, and I could not help, at the same time, finding the whole thing irresistibly hilarious. I was feeling the way one feels at school if the teacher's wig goes askew. I had to share my enjoyment, so I got up, and walking backward so I wouldn't miss anything, I went to the bathroom to fetch the dog so he too could enjoy the show. I set him on my lap and laughed myself to tears.

He fondly licked my hand.

4

That evening Professor Cerignola took me to an Italian restaurant that looked like an English pub, with wood panelling, low ceilings, hunting scenes. Outside the entrance hung a wrought-iron sign showing a woodpecker hard at work drilling a hole in an oak tree.

We ordered *fusilli Amarcord*, and then *artichokes alla giudia, brasato al barolo,* a plum torte.

I said that perhaps I had found someone who could put me in touch with Mrs. Schelucci.

"Is it really that important?"

I knew it must have seemed like a childish whim.

"I thought you'd understand," I said.

The professor smiled. He was charming after all. He was taking me to dinner at all the best restaurants. If only I had given him some encouragement, he would have made an undoubtedly interesting offer. Perhaps, I thought, I should give him a chance to talk.

"I do," he answered, "but perhaps it wouldn't be a bad idea if you were to give a plausible answer when Mr. Shell asks the same question."

The *fusilli Amarcord* was overcooked and overdressed with mushrooms, asparagus, pine nuts, anchovies, basil, artichokes. Why, in the name of God, do you Americans throw ingredients into your sauces with the same indiscriminate abundance of tossing your waste into the garbage can? Who told you to unload the contents of the fridge into your pasta? You'll probably say: "But I ate that at an Italian restaurant." Fine, but I assure you that in the whole of Italy—islands included, from Aosta to Trapani—you won't find a restaurant—or a home—where they offer you such an unappetizing jumble.

"I'll tell him the truth," I answered. "I'll tell him that I must locate the only living person who knew me as a child to ask about something extremely important only she could know. We're in America. If you ask someone to see you, sooner or later they'll see you, and if you ask a reasonable question, sooner or later you'll get a polite answer."

"That's one of the things we're trying to get done in Italy. Access for everybody to everything. Access to an answer, whether affirmative, doubtful, or negative. And without special pull to do it."

"That would really be revolutionary."

"The cornerstone of everything. A passport to the next millennium."

The *artichokes alla giudia* turned out to be *alla romana*, except that the edges of the leaves were a bit scorched. And they'd been drenched in an unforgivable anchovy sauce. My mother didn't know the traditional recipe, but Signora Spizzico, a friend of Dr. Paoletti's, had taught me that particular secret of Jewish-Italian cooking.

"I know how to do it better," I said. "Crisp on the outside, soft on the inside. As golden as sunflowers. And not oily. You know," I added, "I ask myself now and then if it wouldn't have been wonderful to be a great cook. A professional cook, I mean. Feeding people is like giving love . . . I feel it must be a rewarding life for someone who offers a perfect dish to thousands of strangers. A professional satisfaction, and a kind of erotic thrill, too."

"And do you think you'd have wound up being a cook if your mother had allowed you to be left-handed?"

"Perhaps. Or perhaps I would have marched side by side with Cesare on his road to success, and now I'd be a tenured professor in Italy. Maybe I'd have loved my husband for his ambition, instead of despising him for his *arrivisme*. Maybe I'd have children. Maybe I'd have been so confident, locked into my identity and my opinions, that I never would have conceived of the Machine."

I gave up on the last tough leaves of my artichoke and looked up at the professor. The other hypotheses hadn't bothered me as much as this one.

"But," I said, "I can't imagine spending my days without my work on the Machine."

His smile broadened as if I were joking.

"You see, professor," I went on, "the Machine is part of a really ambitious plan. Here I am . . ." I was about to say— I would have said, that first evening after the whiskey sour— "Here I am in high heels and a Versace dress, an attractive, radiant, feminine woman who loves to cook . ... " Again I was thinking of myself in the third person: "Martina Satriano has dark, big, even velvety eyes, a beautiful body, soft black curls, and is, besides, a formidable cook, and yet . . ."

I blushed, hidden by the dim candlelight. "I think it will be a revolutionary discovery. I think the contrast of ideas will take place in a totally new way after I've completed my work."

Martina Satriano would be nothing without the Machine. Martina Satriano—with her cute outfits, her daily workouts at the gym, her courses at the university, her tête-à-tête dinners with Jerry Keleti, her occasional love affairs, her laundry in the basement—isn't capable of investing her days with enough life to build memories on. For that, she has to defer everything to a project.

It should have been an unpleasant thought, but I felt it as an intoxicating shot of adrenaline.

"My nights," I said aloud, "all my nights during these two years are stored in the Machine. It's another life, and yet it's mine. Infinite possible lives. And now if I were to discover that I'm a born lefty, everything would have to be multiplied by two, right?

"Your daytime self and all your nighttime selves . . ."

"Both of them doubled. For each a right-handed version that's been active, and a left-handed version that's been latent."

Professor Cerignola nodded sympathetically.

"Do you realize," I went on, "that the minute I succeed in arriving at a coherent theory from all this that's fit to be published, the habit among all of us of opposition, this polemical ferocity that's poisoned the human race since the beginnings of civilization, will no longer make sense? On television we have seen columns of Serb refugees machine-gunned by Croat soldiers, then—more often, actually—Croat civilians machine-gunned by Serb soldiers, just to name two ethnic groups. A while ago we had the same situation with the Hutus and the Tutsis, and who knows whose turn it'll be next year. And it's clear to everybody that if there were initially a motive for such ferocity, it's irrelevant by now. The ferocity now goes on on its own without the need for justification . . . I ask myself, how could such things happen if each of us were forced to see his own beloved individuality like a paper hat picked by chance from the bunch of favors at a carnival ball? If one of those brutes in battle gear could only see his own face, his own ID, his own uniform as the result of a whim of fate? Suppose I can find the words to put in his head a tiny doubt about his inevitable and unchangeable being . . . How could he cut a baby in half just because it's the child of Serbs or Croats or Muslims?"

The Professor didn't answer for a while. Then he said: "And this thanks to the theory of the multiple identity?"

So said it sounded like nonsense.

"It's not really multiple identity. Identity is only one, but behind, in its shadow, stand all the others that could have been and weren't . . . And it will not be a theory. I know I used the word myself, for lack of a better one, but it's not what I really have in mind. I would like to express my thought, if I succeed in grabbing it, in a way that will speak to the heart of people." I lifted my glass as in a toast. "I don't want to be convincing, I want to be disarming."

The professor too raised his glass and touched mine. "It's a grand project, no doubt." He sounded so forced and false that I felt sure of his intention to please me at any cost. "I think you should continue your work in Italy, with all the financing you need. And certain that it would be presented to the whole world with the importance it deserves."

I was dizzy with excitement. The results of my work presented all over the world, in Italy, above all. In Italy, where my family had toiled for centuries, where I was born, where I had worked and studied without sparing myself. In Italy, where there had been no place for me. Should I consider this a proposal? I hoped so.

I wanted to say yes. I didn't say no. It was late and we arranged to meet for dinner the next night.

Asparagus Soufflé

I

I'm wearing a black bathing suit with white polka dots. I'm heading toward a swimming pool with lots of other people. First the road runs between two laurel bushes that are very close, forcing us to pass through in single file. Then we find ourselves at the foot of a wide staircase. We still proceed one behind the other. The stairs keep going and get steeper. I tell myself the effort is pointless because there can't possibly be a swimming pool at the top—not full in any case—since water tends naturally to flow downward. So I change direction and walk toward the capital city. Now I'm in a room shaped like an amphitheater and full of students. I'm a student, too. The queen arrives wearing a Pierrette costume of white silk with black pompons. When she passes by, she smiles at me very sweetly. I respond with a cold nod. Only afterward, when she's gone by, do I regret it. "You're always so kind to everybody," I say to myself, "how nasty of you to treat her that way just because she's the queen." I realize that I'm still wearing a bathing suit. I take it off and go sit on the dais, my legs spread apart in front of the class. The students file by, have a good look at my crotch, and take notes.

I had set my alarm for an hour earlier. I didn't play bridge. I bolted down my breakfast while dressing. I thought back on the dream only after I was in the subway. Apart from the strange shamelessness of the ending, a very wise dream. Why, in fact, not smile at the queen? Why, also, should I say no to Professor Cerignola when and if he were to make a proposal?

Was it a curse due to an original twist—to the fact that I was not the person I was meant to be—that forced me to be so damned unnatural and not smile at the queen? Or, alternatively, keep my icy face, totally convinced I had done the right thing?

Or was it, on the contrary, a gift of fate that would allow me to extract from my Machine the formula for a new world, the solution for unwinding the springs of rage, transforming intolerance into doubt, anticipating it in everyone's conscience, securing it somewhere safe from where it could no longer inflict injustices, abuses, massacres?

But it was as if I were in a movie with the sound track out of sync, because the images that accompanied my thoughts were those of Costantino's body. I was lying on the moss carpet of the Elephants' Ballroom, looking up at him as he stood astride my hips, slim and tanned like a prehistoric figure painted on the walls of a cave. Or I was watching him as he crossed the clearing to get a water bottle from our knapsack. I can't tell you how fascinating it was, the way he wore his nudity with such simple assurance. It's not a fit subject for a lesson, and I couldn't find the right words. You—you boys, self-assured, brazen—looking at me from behind the shield of your leather jackets, jeans, boots; you're eighteen, twenty. How do you walk when you cross a room naked and somebody's watching you? Do you hide your sex with your hands, do you hunch over as if you were apologizing for having a body? Or, worse, do you strut? Do you pose? I ask you this, because, after Costantino, none of the men I saw under similar circumstances knew how to move like him.

But, of course, neither did I have the same self-assurance in their presence that I had with Costantino. With him around I trusted my body. I was beautiful, because I was so for him. I was unique, because I was so for him. And vice versa. The fact is he knew I loved him and I knew he loved me. We both knew because we let love shine through each gesture, sound through each word. We never thought we had to put on the brakes. We weren't afraid to let go. So never was anything said or done between us that contradicted the plain truth of our mutual love.

Is such spontaneous, unsophisticated sureness possible between two adults? I doubt it. But, as I told you, I'm not an expert. Forget it.

*   *   *

The other thought that kept me company during the subway ride was Professor Cerignola. What point had I got to with him? He hadn't told me anything specific. He was hovering over me in concentric circles, drawing closer and closer. "Would you like to go on with your work in Italy?" Didn't he mean that, more or less, last night? Should I consider it a proposal? Maybe, I thought. But how would I be expected to work? Under what conditions? What would be demanded from me in return?

I unlocked the door to the building housing our department. It was deserted. I read until the early risers among the students started popping into my office. I dispatched them quickly, without giving them much attention or time, I'm sorry to say. I postponed an appointment. By the time I went to class, I had already gained three free hours. At eleven thirty-two, I went through the subway turnstile; at eleven forty-five I was pressing the button on the elevator that would take me up to the White Eagle office on the thirty-fourth floor. Miss Massey was at the receptionist's desk and let me go in immediately.

Mr. Shell's office was very large. An enormous expanse of windows facing south opened on to a limitless view, from the Empire State and Chrysler buildings in the foreground all the way down to the World Trade Center. Mr. Shell's profile, as he sat behind his desk, was outlined against the glare from the windows.

"Please have a seat," he said.

I sat in front of him.

"I took the liberty of coming here to ask you something that will seem nonsensical," I began. I was nervous. All those skyscrapers seemed to be scattered about as if a set designer had been commissioned to provide Mr. Shell with the proper backdrop.

"Don't worry." His tone was gentle. Perhaps he had even smiled but I couldn't tell for sure because he was sitting in silhouette.

I continued. "You see, I need to find a person, a friend of the family, and perhaps you can direct me to her. I'm Italian; I teach European cultural history at NYU, as I indicated on the questionnaire. The woman I'm looking for is also Italian, she was a friend of my mother's since they were children. I think she saw me being delivered, literally, and I need some information about her."

"I'll be glad to help you. Is she one of our employees? We have some women from Europe on our staff."

His English was better than mine, but he still had a slight accent. I couldn't make out his features, but his voice and manner seemed to belong to a young person.

"No, not an employee. She was the owner of the buildings you replaced with Somerset House. Mrs. Marta Schelucci. Does the name mean anything to you?"

He moved a few papers around on his desk. "Schelucci

. . . of course I remember. Those tenements were the first buildings we bought, long before we tore them down. But . . . I'm sorry, Mrs. Schelucci died many years ago."

"Oh . . ." My eyes filled with tears. Papa under his tractor, Bruno Schelucci in a work accident, Marta Schelucci dead before her time, worn out by overwork. My mother had gone on a few years longer . . . but they hadn't been happy years. One could tell from her desolate house. I hadn't arrived in time to say good-bye to her, I hadn't wound Papa's watch, I hadn't ever gone to visit Mrs. Schelucci.

He could see my tears.

"I'm sorry," he said again. "Was it something important?"

I waved disconsolately; nothing seemed important at that moment. "No . . . I mean, yes, it was important . . . but it isn't that. I should have looked for her right away . . . The Scheluccis were close friends, true friends of my family's. We're from the south, we feel these things, but I kept putting it off and then forgot about it. It serves me right." I sighed. "I wanted to ask her something about my early childhood . . . Something only she could have known. It was important, actually."

"Too bad," he said in a gentle voice. "Besides," he added, "Who knows, after so many years, if she'd remember the time she was in Lucania. Many immigrants prefer to forget."

2

On my way home I got off the train at the stop before my usual one and walked for a bit. I was thinking of my mother and of Marta Schelucci. I was thinking about Costantino, and of our fathers, both killed in work accidents.

I almost tripped on the body of the tramp. He was lying in the middle of the sidewalk, face down, a few yards from my doorway. By now I was used to seeing bundles along the street that look like piles of throw-away rags. Ever since I'd arrived in New York, whenever I walked by them, I had learned to accept the fact that those shapeless heaps were human beings sleeping there. They had a technique for surviving; they knew the best places to find shelter; they had a special skill for putting together plastic bags and cardboard boxes. I gradually began to walk by them without feeling uneasy. There wasn't anything I could do for them, after all. That's how it was. That's how life is. New York is the center of the world, a magnet that draws everybody, even those who will never make it. After they get over their drunken stupor, all those rag heaps will regain, for a brief while, human shape and make their way to the Salvation Army for a bowl of soup. Then over to a subway entrance or to a bank to rattle their cups for some change.

And then all over again. Perhaps no one could do anything about it. Certainly not I.

This man was a tramp, too, it was obvious, but it didn't seem he was lying there just to sleep it off. I was convinced he had collapsed. Maybe he was dying, alone, on the sidewalk. Passing people skirted around him. I turned to a young black man who was swaying as he walked, his ears plugged into a Walkman.

"Shouldn't we do something?" I asked.

"I beg your pardon?"

"Would you mind turning that thing off a minute?" He unplugged his left earpiece and stood there, still swaying to the music. From the small earpiece dangling on his chest you could hear the thin rock beat. A hissing sound. A bunch of mosquitoes playing—I think—*Real Man.*

I pointed to the bundle on the sidewalk. "Shouldn't we do something?"

He looked surprised and stopped dancing. "What did you say?"

"I think this man's ill"

"Naw, he's drunk." He stuck the earpiece back into his ear, soldering the music to his brain. He looked as if he had disappeared into a container. He and his Walkman had become a smooth, uninterrupted casing without a single opening. An egg. He went on his way, still undulating to the music.

I leaned over the tramp. "Hey," I said.

He didn't move. I didn't want to touch him. "Are you OK?"

People kept passing by, ignoring me and the tramp. I mustered the courage to turn him partially so I could see his face.

"Are you OK?" I repeated. This time he heard me.

"Call the cops," he said.

I turned to a woman with a dog. "Please call the police," I pleaded. "This man's sick and wants me to call the police."

"Call the cops," the man repeated.

"Call them yourself," the woman said to me.

"All right, I will. Stay here with him."

The dog started sniffing at the tramp, his friendly tail wagging. The woman gave him a sharp tug and walked away without answering me.

I didn't know the phone number for the police. I had never needed to call the police. Was there an emergency number? Did I have to call the local precinct? Which was my local precinct? There was a telephone booth at the corner, but no phone directory.

"Hold on," I assured the tramp. "I'll be right back."

Mr. Serrano was at the reception desk. I smiled at him. I knew he liked me and would listen.

"Please do me a favor, call the police. A man is out there lying on the sidewalk . . . he's been taken ill."

"What man?"

"Well, a homeless, I think."

He looked puzzled. Like the young man with the Walkman and the woman with the dog. I was embarrassing everybody. I was a foreigner not going by the rules.

I remembered the first time I was invited to the dean's house for dinner. The menu began with soup and ended with dessert. The dessert spoon was set to the right of the plate next to the knife, the soup spoon behind the plate next to the glasses. The opposite of how it's done in Europe. I was full of doubts. Take up the wrong spoon from the right place or the right spoon from the wrong place? I decided to begin the meal—an awful one—by using the tiny dessert spoon for the soup, and as a result had to dig into my little ball of strawberry sherbet with the monstrous soup spoon.

And I went on till the end of that unhappy evening, knowing that I was moving helplessly from mistake to mistake, because the way the cutlery was laid out indicated a general logic in the whole matter that seemed opposite to the one I had been taught. Who was to tell me the rest also had not been reversed? What other blunders had I made with the glasses, the napkin, the conversation, the good-byes? I tried watching the others in the candlelight, squinting through the centrepieces of freesia and anemones. It was only years later that I learned that the dean, then a bachelor, hired untrained students who performed their task in a juvenile impromptu style. I also learned that ordinarily place settings were laid out the same in America as in Italy, but in the meantime I had come across other notable differences.

"Relax, ma'am," the doorman said. "Calm down. As soon as he's past his hangover, he'll be all right. Let him be. When he wakes up, the first thing he'll do is ask you for money."

He was like the others. I stood there, my smile glued to my face, trying to make sense of it all. It was like waking up in the cold shadows of the universe rather than in my own bed. I recalled something Jerry Keleti often used to say: "We're on an uncontrollable raft drifting toward the second millennium. And on this wretched raft there's not even room for everybody."

I said, "Let me have the phone, I'll call them." There was a limit to my willingness to adapt to the local etiquette. My zeal to conform didn't go beyond a certain point. I wouldn't christen my children, if I had had any, Savile, Kenneth, or Dexter. I wouldn't leave a man to die alone on the sidewalk.

The operator switched me from one number to another until I was connected to the closest emergency service.

"Stay with him and don't move him," the paramedic said. "We'll be right there."

I handed the phone back to Mr. Serrano without a word of thanks and ran out.

The dying man had disappeared. I asked the passers-by

if they had seen him. "Who?" they asked, looking embarrassed.

"The homeless man. The man lying right here on the sidewalk."

They shook their heads no, shrugged their shoulders.

For a moment I thought of taking off before the ambulance got there. Mr. Serrano was standing by the door, looking in my direction. I could just imagine the expression on his face. I forced myself not to be irritated for being made a fool of by the tramp's miraculous cure. I tried to feel charitable and positive about his recovery. I waited, standing in the middle of the sidewalk trying not to look too stupid.

There were three of them in the ambulance, two paramedics and the driver.

"I'm very sorry," I said, "when I got back here, he'd gone. He really seemed very ill . . . I've bothered you over nothing. I'm terribly sorry."

"You did right by calling us. You don't know how many people die on the streets because nobody wants to get involved . . . or because nobody really cares." One of the paramedics was a black man, the other white. The driver was Chinese. All three of them shook my hand. "Have a good day, lady. Nice meeting you."

3

He took me to a famous Italian restaurant on East Sixty-eighth Street with a French name and an international menu.

"I made reservations," he assured me, "because the place is always full."

The owner himself, smiling, came forward to greet us and showed us to a corner table.

We ordered an entrecote with truffles and an asparagus soufflé.

The dining room was crowded. Many of the diners seemed to be Italians, very well dressed and deeply conscious of the effect they were making: the women bronzed by sun lamps or the tropical sun, all of them blonde and forever ageless, clones based on a prototype created jointly by Valentino, Vergottini, and Slim Fast. The men were somewhat more differentiated, some of them being fat, others bald.

It was quieter in the dining room than in most restaurants. Maybe the people were speaking in more subdued tones or they had less to say to each other. I too had little more to talk about with Professor Cerignola. I realized that he, without appearing to, got me to say more than if he had submitted me to an interrogation. His first hints were vague, and even on the preceding evening he hadn't really made me, all told, a concrete proposal I could accept or refuse. His intention in our meetings up to that point was obviously to get to know me before deciding whether to make a real offer or not.

As I sipped the vermentino that was served along with a sturgeon pâté, I asked myself a bit anxiously if the offer would ever be made. Up to now, I told myself, he hasn't dismissed me. I realized I desperately wanted to be invited back to Italy, to hear an offer being made to me of a prestigious position.

"We need," the professor was saying, "someone who can break up the perversely homogeneous ways of thinking in our country."

"Oh?"

He sighed and waved his hands about. "It's something in the air. We're almost no longer aware of it. Last week, just before I left Italy, I happened to be watching a talk show on TV. One of the most famous and authoritative architects in Italy was on it, the editor of a major architectural magazine, a small, wiry, spiteful man . . . charming in his way. At a certain point he announced, 'I've never published a single post-modern building in my magazine.' You see, as if he had performed a voodoo rite. Like erasing something, putting it out of existence. He said it quite proudly, certain of winning the audience's approval."

"And you don't think he did?"

"Oh no, he did. And that's the point. As I've been saying, intolerance is a virtue in Italy. We're living through the post-Freud, post-Einstein, post-Picasso, post-Schoenberg, post-Joyce era, and yet we continue holding on to our anachronistic belief in certainty, in absolute values, in an immutable morality. That view of the world was tossed out the door a long time ago by the culture of our time. But we let it back in through the window, reaffirming the old single-minded system of fixed imperatives that belonged to the past and the idea that the universe is an ordered system endowed with meaning. We say of anyone who thinks differently from us that 'he's an imbecile' or 'he sold out.'"

"It's not too different here," I said.

"My dear, much, much different. Italian culture has been nourished, raised, and brought into the twentieth century by a nurse called the Catholic Church: we have to struggle harder than most others to get free from the Truth with a capital T. And we resist adapting to a relative universe more fiercely than others. We accepted fascism with unforgivable enthusiasm, and when it was finished, we built the strongest communist party outside the Warsaw Pact. And we lived through both -isms with the tenacity and intolerance of Absolute Conviction."

I gathered he had stopped wringing information out of me. He was doing the talking now.

"To paraphrase Pascal," he continued, "today, *il faut courir le risque du scepticisme*. The whole world's beginning to do it, and even if we're trailing behind, we must also. We can't go on taking the old Truths with a capital T apart and replacing them with new Truths, always with a capital T. Truths, like Values, can be maintained safely only if they're written in small letters. Otherwise they will always stir up war. We have to learn to accept the fact that there are conflicting ideas, interests, tastes, egos. Even—pace the Master Architect—opposing architectural ideals. We must grow up."

They brought us the entrecote.

"When you talk about the perverse homogeneity of thinking in Italy, do you mean that everybody adheres to these Truths? That's not the case. It's said we've never succeeded in having a stable government precisely because of so many radically disparate opinions."

He shifted about in his chair and—for the first time—spoke to me in an irritated tone.

"I meant 'everybody' in a general sense, obviously. 'Everybody,' like when the smart set says 'Everybody's at Salzburg this summer,' or the locals gathering at the village café say 'Everybody's been to bed with Rosina.' To each one inside a big or little 'Everybody,' nothing exists outside of it . . . I think it's Romeo who says 'There's no world outside the walls of Verona.' There are many Everybodys in every society."

"You mean intellectuals, businessmen, judges, professionals, bankers . . ."

"Not exactly. It's a matter of transversal—as they say nowadays—Everybodys. In this one intellectuals predominate, in that one taxi drivers . . . so if we give it that meaning, then, yes, everybody adheres. It's a law of physics that's stronger than gravity. The academician who banishes postmodernism from his review has certainly succeeded in banishing it, not from the whole country, but from the minds of those Everybodys who have cultural prestige or would like to have it. Opposing the official mindset is forbidden to the point that Everybody is convinced other ways of thinking don't even exist; other ways are nonthinking. Acknowledging their existence is mortally dangerous. Such as questioning the magical cancellation of postmodernism."

"I've been away from Italy for a long time," I said, "but at university it was the same in my day."

"Did you like it?"

"No, as I've told you. I felt violated precisely because it was such a temptation to become aligned . . . or I felt alone because it was so hard being on the outside . . . I ended up marrying. I got married to overcome the temptation to join the herd and the loneliness I was condemning myself to by not joining. An idiotic decision . . ."

I said to myself, the professor is as sly as a polecat. He came up with this story because he knew I'd go for it. He can't have missed the analogy between what he said tonight and my work on the Machine. Disarming intolerance means making room for a multiplicity of ideas. He knows that perfectly well, but pretends not to. He leaves it up to me to note how easy working together would be. He's decided to ask me to return to Italy, I thought. Tonight he'll tell me what he expects of me.

They brought us two small asparagus soufflés with a fontina sauce. It all tasted very good, but I figured I had eaten as much butter during that one meal as I allowed myself all year.

I couldn't bear waiting any longer to hear a concrete proposal.

"Apropos of what you were saying . . ." I said, "it's curious . . ." I paused to clear my throat.

"My work," I went on, "is designed to allow for a more open comparison of ideas." I realized I was offering myself shamelessly to him. And with such banality besides.

"If they only were ideas," the professor sputtered. He was getting more irritated. "An idea is born again every day because every day it's subject to modifications, contradictions, to evolving. But do we really have ideas? Does our famous architect's idea seem like one to you? We no longer have ideas—only opinions. Those mummified ideas that are called opinions."

It turned out to be a negative evening. The professor was in a bad mood. He did not make me any concrete proposals.

*   *   *

The puppy had behaved. He'd done his duty on the newspapers I had spread in a corner of the bathroom. I let him roam around the apartment while I prepared his bowl. He immediately ran into my room and proudly brought back one of my slippers. It was an emerald green terry mule. I ran to get my Polaroid and snapped two or three shots. I pasted the most charming of them on a sheet of paper and wrote a message: "Cute, loving, and well-trained puppy needs a family." I shut him back into the bathroom with his bowl of food, went to bed.

Porcini and Potatoes

I

I'm in the bathroom in front of the mirror. It's not the usual mirror; this one's much bigger, luminous, rectangular, framed by shelves on which are arranged expensive-looking perfumes, lotions, and beauty creams. The mirror speaks and, after highly praising the quality of the items, announces that they are free. I tell myself I've never believed in the miracles commercials promise, but certainly those products couldn't be bad. I might be able to erase a few years—ten or twelve, maybe. And there's nothing to feel ashamed about, I didn't order them. I'm very excited by the prospect of using those cosmetics. The jars and crystal flacons are delicately colored—peach, aquamarine, mallow—and sparkle on the crystal shelves.

I didn't bother to analyze the dream. I spent an hour at the Health Club and the rest of the morning at school. I had lunch at the cafeteria and started on my way back so that I could be home by three. I stopped to buy milk, croissants, and dog food. I also got a bunch of yellow tulips. Ever since I'd woken up a thought had been running through my mind I couldn't quite get hold of, a doubt, something that didn't jibe. I kept thinking about my visit to the White Eagle office—Miss Massey and her fingernails, the view from the window behind Mr. Shell, our brief conversation—and then from the beginning again. A circular thought, inconclusive and disturbing.

Everything became clear in a flash while I was putting the tulips in the Lucanian pot with the two small handles next to each other on the side.

It was Saturday, the office was surely closed, but Jerry had also given me Mr. Shell's home address. I walked eight blocks west and six north. His address was halfway between the Plaza and the St. Moritz. When the doorman asked whom he should announce, I said boldly, "Martina." He mumbled into the intercom and then said to me, "18L."

He was at home alone; he answered the door himself.

I was standing on the door mat facing him. It was dark in the foyer; once again I had trouble making out his features, but this time it didn't matter.

"Ciao, Costantino," I said. "Why did you pretend you didn't know me?"

He hugged me and gave me a kiss.

From the time we used to embrace under the oak tree at Poggio di Mezzo, I had grown perhaps six inches. He had grown more than that, but my high heels made up the difference. Our limbs fit the same way they used to. I recognized every inch of his body, strong and lean, pressed against mine.

"You brought up Lucania at a certain point." I said. "Something like 'Who knows if she remembered Lucania.' I hadn't mentioned it. I said that your mother, like me, was from the south, but I didn't mention any particular region. It was a mistake. Or wasn't it?"

"I don't know. Maybe I wanted you to recognize me."

"Is it true your mother's dead?"

"Yes, it's been almost twenty years."

"I'm sorry. Mine, too, a week ago."

"I know. I'm sorry."

"You know?"

"Yes, I know. I've never lost track of you."

"What do you mean?"

"I've always been kept posted about you. About you, about your family. I know a lot of things."

"A lot of things?"

"My mother . . . you know what a bigot she was—much as yours, however. As soon as she made some money she started sending the priest in Nugola an offering every Christmas and Easter. And when he wrote to thank her he always added a complete report about all the villagers, particularly about those who were from Lucania like us;

about you more than all. Then, when Mamma died I went on sending money and getting the news. It's very simple."

"I don't understand you. In all these years you haven't lost track of me, but why didn't you try to see me?"

He took me by the hand and led me to the window. He still had that gypsy face, but with a few lines in it, and his hair had a touch of gray. Some people become someone else as they age: he hadn't. He was still my Costantino, only twenty-five years older. A wide mouth, marked cheekbones, his somewhat protuberant teeth. I recognized the face with the ready smile from my dream of the young man on the motorcycle.

"I kept an eye on you, in a certain sense. But I had cut loose from the old days and didn't want to meet up with you. I had succeeded in distancing myself from sad memories, I didn't want anything to attach me to the past again . . . You know, I'm not the only one in America who wants to forget. The misery, the discrimination. Things here are easy for Roman princesses, for the Milanese fashion designers. Much less, believe me, for a guy that lands in this country penniless from southern Italy. Now I'm Kevin Shell, and I can look at all this in a different way."

"Do you remember Carmelina?"

"Of course."

"She's married."

"Yes, I know that, too."

"She's also changed her name. Now she's Milly. Carmelina had too much of a southern ring to it for someone who's so keen about being married to a dentist from Livorno."

I told him what little he didn't know about my sister, her children, my teaching post at the university. He told me in greater detail the story I'd already heard from the dressmaker, Mrs. Guerriero.

"Schelucci didn't work. You can imagine how they pronounced it. And Costantino became Kevin. Shorter, easier. Although, at this point it doesn't matter anymore."

"It doesn't matter?"

"No, I'm leaving. I sold my share of the White Eagle. I've got rid of everything—this apartment won't be mine by next month. I'm going back to Italy, starting all over again. I've invested my assets so that I can live the life I want to."

"Such as?"

"Nothing special. I like soccer, I want to see Juventus play on Sundays. I want to go skiing in the Alps. I want to have a little weekend place on Capraia island and a sailboat docked in the harbor. I want to live on a small continent, where everything is close. I want to be a short distance from Paris, London, Berlin, Vienna. I want to be able to visit the Prado, if I choose, and be home for dinner. I want to go back to my country, and I can, now. Does that sound crazy?"

I didn't answer. He was still holding my hand; he lifted it and kissed my fingertips, as he had when we were kids.

"But now, more than anything else, I want to enjoy seeing you again."

Then we fell silent. It wasn't possible to pick up where we had left off twenty-five years ago. I knew that nothing in his life, as in mine, would ever be as natural and perfect as our taking each other's clothes off, as my exploring his body and his exploring mine with our eyes, our tongues, our fingers; nothing as simple and sweet as our cautious love-making. Nothing would ever give me a greater sense of security than the hand that grasped mine and helped me onto the rotting platform in the crotch of the tallest oak, where years ago hunters lay in wait for the wood pigeons to fly over. No act would ever inspire in me as much confidence, friendship, tenderness as those small gestures of his I've recalled so often—the handkerchief wrapped around a cut on my knee, his sweater laid out on the ground so I could rest my head on it. I've said "I love you" to very few men and to none with the same conviction.

But that was twenty-five years ago. Authentic, natural, and perfect things were part of a lost age and couldn't be relived except in an artificial, unnatural, faulted way. We waited a moment, as if expecting an outside force that would make everything right again. Then Costantino said, "You know, there's a place in Central Park where mushrooms grow by the hatful."

2

We went there with a Saks Fifth Avenue shopping bag. "I go jogging here in the morning," he said. We went into the park and headed west toward the rise near Seventieth Street. The mushrooms weren't growing by the hatful, but we did find five beautiful porcini in a small clearing. It was like being back at Poggio di Mezzo

We kept looking but didn't find more until it was time for me to get ready for my usual appointment. "I have to be going," I said. "I'm meeting someone for dinner tonight who's trying to get me to go back to Italy." As we left the park I told him about the feelers Professor Cerignola was putting out. We waited for the light to change at the corner by the St. Moritz. "It's wonderful, this happening right now," Costantino said.

"Right now?"

"Now that I'm going, too. Now that we've found each other again."

"You mean now that I've flushed you out."

"I'm only too grateful that it happened."

The light had changed to "walk" but we lingered. Costantino laid the bag of mushrooms on the park wall and put his hands on my shoulders. "It's true, I never looked for you, but you didn't look for me either when you came to

America. Perhaps you wanted to break with the past, too. But now, here we are with a bag of mushrooms. A new beginning."

I knew it wouldn't be that simple. We could believe it while we were like children looking for mushrooms under the oaks in Central Park, but as soon as we crossed the street everything would return to being difficult, awkward, unnatural. The simplest thing to do was to get away with the excuse I had an appointment with Professor Cerignola.

"He hasn't proposed anything in particular. In any case, I must be ready in an hour and a half."

He picked up the bag and led me by the elbow back to the corner. "Not tonight, it's out of the question. You'll have to phone him that you can't make it."

The light went back to "walk". We raced across: he was no longer a boy looking for mushrooms but an executive who knew what he wanted and how to get it. He took long strides; I struggled to keep up with him. "I can't phone him. I don't know which hotel he's staying at."

"Don't worry. I'll find out; give me ten minutes."

Five minutes was more like it. He was at the Pierre. "I'll ring his room," the hotel operator said.

He was in.

"We'll have to put off our dinner. I can't make it. Is tomorrow night all right, at the same time?"

He didn't object. I hung up, and it was as if I had lost hold of a life belt.

Now Costantino and I had the whole evening before us, and maybe the whole night. And the next day being Sunday, with no plausible excuses about work, we'd face endless hours until my date with Professor Cerignola at six. An awful stretch of time, awkward, perhaps boring, frightening for the possibilities for disappointment. I turned toward him and realized he was thinking the same thing. We were standing facing each other on a carpet I imagined was very valuable. If it had been the moss-covered ground of the Elephants' Ball and if we were twenty years younger, I could have confided to him the professional frustrations I had experienced in Italy, the minor success I had achieved in America, the great temptation Professor Cerignola was serving up to me every night along with lobster and *tarte Tatin*. If we could have gone back to that time and place I'd have been able to share my thoughts with him. And being there, possessing both the simplicity of youth and the wisdom of age, I could also have shared my body with him, and he would have been at ease with both.

But the time was different, and the place, and us. I couldn't unload on him problems that weren't his, demand his undivided attention. If it had been back then and there I would have touched him, undressed him, without pausing to think how much pleasure I'd be giving him, or how much he'd be giving me. Today I was asking myself who would make the first move, and what sort of move would it be. I was very aware that my body wasn't what it was before. Trim, thanks to the health club, but hardly an adolescent's. And I looked at his body, wondering if it would be strange to me. I worried about what he would think. I worried about how I would feel.

I asked, "Do you have any calamint in the house?"

He laughed. "I don't even know if there's any salt. I always eat out."

"Then let's go cook the mushrooms at my place."

We left his apartment, relieved as if we had been reprieved.

The puppy had lapped up his bowl of Alpo. I threw away the newspapers he had soiled and changed his water. "He's a beautiful little dog," Costantino said. He bent over to pick him up.

"I have to find a new master for him." I uncorked a bottle of Barbaresco and began to peel the potatoes. I made Costantino sit where I could see him. The dog was standing on his hind legs on his lap, leaning against his chest, eagerly licking his chin.

"I'll give you a hand," said Costantino.

"Stay right there. I like to cook on my own." It was my turn now to stand against the light, with my back to the kitchen window. I wondered how much of time's ravages he had already noticed in me. My skin wasn't the same, and my hair would have had a strand or two of grey if it weren't for Miracle Rinse. But my body had aged well, keeping the right proportions, I told myself. I had good teeth, I told myself, my breasts didn't sag.

I cubed the potatoes and put them in a terracotta pot with a little olive oil, and tossed them with my hands. I put them to cook on a mid-size burner and turned up the flame. I had gone looking all over, including Queens, Brooklyn, and the Bronx to find a stove with different size burners, each with variable control from high to low. I wrote to my mother about this gastronomic barbarity in America, where they try to cook everything with the same heat. She called Dr. Paoletti and Signor Ceccarelli, and they were all scandalized.

Martina Satriano, I thought, is preparing mushrooms and potatoes for her Costantino because she knows she can do it well. She should go up to him, take off her clothes, take off his, brush up against his body, learn to know him again with her eyes, her hands, her tongue. But she isn't sure she can do that as gracefully as she did when she was thirteen. Actually she is certain of the opposite.

I cleaned the mushrooms and lined them up on a towel. I stirred the potatoes that were beginning to brown. I turned the flame down to low. I went to the sideboard in the living room for a tablecloth and spread it on the table. I brought over two blue candle holders with yellow candles in them. Costantino watched me through the open door.

"You have a beautiful walk," he said. "I'd recognize you by your walk even if you wore a mask. When you came to meet me at the Elephant's Ball, I wouldn't see you until the last minute. You'd slip through the woods silently, like an Indian. Then suddenly you were there at the edge of the clearing. And you'd come toward me as if wafted by a breeze."

I went back to the kitchen, cut up the mushrooms and stirred the potatoes again, moving the pot over to the small burner and setting the flame to low.

He added, "When I got to America I wrote you, but decided not to mail the letters. I made the mistake of reading them over again, and they seemed so stupid . . ."

"It's not easy to write love letters without sounding ridiculous." I hated the sanctimonious tone in my voice. Martina Satriano and her Costantino are circling about, I said to myself. But I went on, "And even talking about love without seeming stupid is rather difficult." Perhaps it was fairer to say he was circling because I was keeping him at a distance, I thought. I started to cook the mushrooms in a wide frying pan over the largest burner with the flame set on high. I went out on the terrace to pick some calamint and scattered about ten of the little leaves on the mushrooms.

"In five minutes," I said. "Put the dog down, wash your hands, and bring the plates to the table." He did so while I kept an eye on the pots. He lit the candles. He too had a pleasing walk. He was wearing a pair of black corduroy pants, a chequered shirt under a camel-hair sweater. He was as slim as when he was young. Besides, I told myself, he's only forty-four.

The other Martina Satriano, the left-handed one, I said to myself, would have already put an end to this absurdly embarrassing situation. I knew what she would have done, but I couldn't figure out how she'd do it with . . . *naturalezza*, how does one say it in English? Naturalness? Naturality? One or the other might be in the dictionary, but what unnatural sounds. I've never heard anyone say either. Left-handed Martina wouldn't have worried about the dictionary. She would have made the right move . . . She would have done the right thing without observing herself as she did it.

I emptied the mushrooms into the pot with the potatoes, raised the heat, stirred it for a minute, and then brought it to table. We sat across from one another. We ate, drank wine. When we were finished and sitting back in our chairs, the puppy went to the bathroom to get his bowl. He brought it to us between his teeth, then let it fall at our feet with a great clatter. I fed him some of the leftovers. He ate them and then curled up under the table, going to sleep instantly.

"Look how happy he is," Costantino said.

Dusk was darkening the East River. The lights in Queens and Manhattan criss-crossed as they reflected on the water. The barges slipped by, their wakes multiplying the reflections.

"What did you want from my mother?" asked Costantino.

I told him. "Do you know," I added, "do you know if it's true I was born left-handed?"

He didn't. I explained to him why I wanted to find out. I described the Machine to him. We went to sit on the couch next to each other. I continued about the multiplication of personalities in dreams, about the virtual I. I was moving us off the dangerous ground of the past. It was as assuring as talking to Professor Cerignola.

"If I succeed in proving—or better yet, in making it truly felt—that the real I is only one of innumerable virtual I's, the one, among many, that by chance came into being . . . Do you realize that? How will people go on being so damned in love with themselves, intolerant of their neighbors, hard-headed about opinions, feelings, tastes that are theirs only as the result of a very banal quirk of fate? How can we go on cutting each other's throats? Or we will, but only from greed, dear old greed, so natural a drive to violence. We'll kill one another to steal an inheritance, a suitcase full of money, a client, a pair of shoes, a piece of bread: fair enough."

"Fair enough?"

"Natural, let's say. It won't be pleasant but it will be right from a logical point of view. Greed and violence are blood sisters, how can it surprise us if they go hand in hand? At least we'll have put an end to senseless aggression moti- vated by ideology, religion, morals, aesthetics . . . We'll have put an end to that stupid, fierce, reciprocal rage that for years has been touted as a sublime ethical value under the name of capacity for indignation. What is more stupid than the much celebrated capacity for indignation?"

We had walked in the Park, we had cooked, we had eaten. Now we were sitting side by side on the sofa, and the only thing I could do was build a wall of words between me and Costantino.

"You mean that you don't believe in Truth with a capital *T*, I suppose."

"Funny, Professor Cerignola was saying the same thing yesterday. I don't know. I believe in truth, but not in capitals, don't you see? I fear capital letters. The work I'm doing has exactly that purpose: unmasking the perverse use of the capital *T* in truth, of the capital *E* in ego. And the capital *I* in I, isn't it ridiculous? And breaking up actual identity into many virtual identities is the means of getting there."

"Watch out," he said.

"Watch out?"

He came closer, put his arm around me. "It could be dangerous. You might.. how to put it . . . fall apart. Not be able to hold together anymore."

He pulled me to him, kissed my hair. "Look, you're you . . . I know you. I recognize you. You're none of those countless people you could have been. You're you and I love you. I've kept away from you, that's true, but as it happens I'm here now and I don't ever want to lose you again. So take care not to get lost. Not to lose sight of yourself, do you understand? Stay in touch with yourself."

He kissed me again. The wax from the nondrip candles was dripping on the tablecloth. I stood up and blew them out. I turned on the light. It was ten o'clock. "You should go," I said. He didn't object.

At the door, I hugged him and kissed him hard on the mouth. Suddenly his arms were around me.

"Martina . . ."

"No, please go."

I cleared the table, straightened up. The dog was awake again and following my every move.

While I was picking up his bowl to take back to the bathroom, I heard Costantino's voice again: "Look how happy he is." His voice, his eyes, the five words, the exact intonation. Sitting, relaxed, with his left arm on the back of the chair, his long legs crossed. "Look how happy he is." No one after Costantino had been important to me.

Through the open window I could hear the subdued hum of the traffic. The last of the weekenders were heading up FDR Drive on their way to their houses in Connecticut.

I took two sleeping pills, turned out the light and went to bed. I decided, for that night, not to shut the puppy into the bathroom. I turned on the Machine and cried myself to sleep.

Sunday: Rhubarb Sorbet

I

On Sundays the Machine was programmed to tape dreams at eight. I woke up much earlier, turned on the coffee maker and the toaster oven. I canceled the alarm and taping programs. I didn't remember my dream.

The puppy came up to me and I gave him a piece of croissant. He devoured it, then he tried to jump on my bed, but when he realized I wasn't going to help him, he resigned himself and curled up on my slippers.

I had a quick breakfast. The day was warm and clear. I put on a bathing suit under my gym outfit and dashed up to the health club to avoid answering the phone in case Costantino called. I stayed on the roof deck for a long while taking the sun. Then I went into the health club and did the rounds of the equipment, one after the other. Many of the tenants were away for the weekend, and I had the whole gym to myself.

I took a shower and then went out to shop in my sweat

suit without stopping by my apartment to change. The city was deserted. I bought the Sunday *Times* and read the front section over a coffee in the supermarket cafeteria. I went back to my apartment in time to catch the news from Italy that's on TV at twelve-thirty on Sundays.

The dog heard me come in and greeted me joyously with my green slipper in his mouth. He hadn't done anything in the apartment. I changed the newspapers on the floor, set out his food, and let him roam while the water for the pasta was coming to the boil on the stove. I sat at the foot of the bed and turned on the TV to watch the Italian news. The commercials were still on. I pressed the mute button.

In the moments between the cry of a gull and the sound of a distant horn, the room was filled with that dead silence that happens in New York only on Sunday mornings when those going away for the weekend have gone and no one is returning yet. I closed my eyes and crossed my legs in the lotus position as I prepared to do a couple of relaxing exercises. I took a deep breath, but I suddenly opened my eyes and uncrossed my legs. A tiny sound was coming from the Machine that could only be detected in that dead silence.

I was immediately aware of what had happened. I had anticipated electrical outages and surges, storms, my own distractions, an overheated toaster or coffee maker, and had installed safety measures in the Machine to avoid any damage.

What I hadn't anticipated was a puppy roaming uncontrolled around the apartment. I hadn't foreseen that he'd get up on his hind legs looking for some croissant crumbs and put his paws on the tape deck's keyboard.

I saw what had happened but didn't realize the extent of the disaster. I monitored the tape, fast forwarding and reversing it, but there were only the sounds of the apartment or traffic noises coming in the window.

The battery of tapes my friend the technician had mounted on the Machine could record for eight hours and then, by auto reversing at the end, could tape over what had been recorded. The puppy must already have been at the Machine while I was clearing up the kitchen the night before. The tape now contained night noises, the wailing of sirens, early morning chirping, my footsteps across the floor, the rustling of the bed sheets or the curtains stirred by the breeze, the clicking back and forth of the bathroom door, my footsteps again and finally silence . . . silence.

The noises and the silence had filled in the unused tape and then had poured on the reversed side, erasing nearly eight hours of recorded material, the equivalent of two years' worth of dreams.

As I mechanically continued to hit the forward and reverse buttons, I kept my eye on the TV screen but didn't take off the mute. The commentators mouthed silently. Then someone appeared who might have been the Minister of

Justice. Watching the news as I did only a couple of times a week, I wasn't up on identifying faces. Then the Chief Justice of the Constitutional Court appeared, or was it he? Then a leader of a coalition party, then a leader of the opposition, or vice versa. A political commentator came on, staring straight ahead, probably connected via satellite.

I unplugged the Machine, like a doctor unplugging a dead patient from his life support system. Now there was absolute silence in the room. The chief figures in Italian politics continued to exchange accusations of fraud and deceit without making a sound. I had been close to making a great discovery that would have acknowledged the validity of the differing viewpoints and made it possible for them to work together for the common good. But a clumsy puppy had spoiled it all.

Yes, I could have begun all over again.

I turned up the volume. "I am perfectly secure in the knowledge I've done nothing wrong," one of them who looked familiar was saying. "This whole affair is ridiculous to say the least. The accusations made against me are totally groundless."

I wasn't sure whether it was a judge, a minister, a member of the opposition or of the majority. His statement didn't help in identifying him because I'd heard the same thing recently from almost all the people in public life. And even the others would have said it eventually. The hunt for skeletons in everyone's closet, now at full tilt, would never end. And anyone not participating in the game was considered suspect and labeled a "do-gooder."

What supreme authority could have descended from on high to stop this? And in attempting to do so, who would ever be free of the suspicion that he wanted to preserve an ancient privilege, or create a new one, or even cover up some terrible secret?

I muted the sound again. I didn't think for a moment the dreams that had been erased could be replaced by new ones. I didn't say to myself that the hypothesis of a left-handed self could have led to the completion of my work in a simpler, more forceful way than the Machine could have done.

I did not feel sorry for myself, because I suddenly saw my whole project as an old spinster's game of solitaire, a spinster alone in an self-centered world like Jerry's, sheltered from the judgment of others as his was.

I asked myself what would my father have said if he had been sitting next to me in front of the TV. Would he have continued to believe that each of those characters was right in his own way? Or wouldn't he rather have maintained his tolerant attitude by believing that in any case they were all wrong?

I recalled a long time ago cruelly disabusing my sister Carmelina of her belief in elves, fairies, and knights in shining armor, after which she no longer even believed in the foxes, the storks, and other fabled animals. Would the same thing have happened to him? Was the same thing happening to me? I watched the news program on mute till the end, oppressed by a growing feeling of nausea.

Costantino hadn't phoned, and so I wasn't forced to refuse to see him again. Or if I had agreed to meet him, to temporize awkwardly while I debated what to do. Martina Satriano will remain alone on a fine Sunday morning in her apartment on the East River. She had found again the only man she can love—she herself went looking for him. Then what? Then she cooked for him, ate with him, spoke to him about the Machine, which, in the meantime, died. And this morning she ran out of the house to avoid giving in to the temptation to answer the phone if he called.

Was she happy now that Costantino hadn't called?

She wasn't at all.

I turned off the burner under the pot; the water had almost boiled away. I went out again. Partly on foot and partly by bus I got to Canal Street and then as far as Orchard Street where the fabric stores are located. They were all open even though it was Sunday.

I decided I'd make slipcovers for the chairs and couch. It wasn't such a bad idea to be able to take them off and wash them when necessary. I had them show me roll after roll of fabric. I took some samples. Then I strolled along Houston Street and stopped in at a used furniture store. I bought an old Dutch creamer shaped like a cow.

I went back home, took a shower and dressed for my appointment with Professor Cerignola.

I found a single message on the answering machine, from Costantino. "I don't want to pressure you. Call me if you like."

It was a strange supper. The restaurant was near the World Trade Center. A big, rectangular room with a high ceiling. The waiters in tuxedos, the diners smartly dressed, all very formal.

We ordered oysters, quiche Lorraine, and rhubarb sorbet.

We didn't say much. I didn't want to tell the Professor that all my work on the Machine had been lost. The temptation to accept an offer from him was stronger than ever.

That is, if he still intended to make me one.

The Professor, too, didn't speak much. My mind wandered. Martina Satriano is about to land flat on her rear. Costantino had not really pressured her. And what if he got away? Or if Cerignola didn't make a firm offer? He had had the opportunity to look her over during their meetings. What if he realized that, after all, Professor Martina Satriano, who was totally unknown in Italy, would not have been a feather in his cap? That she wasn't very different from the thousands of dissatisfied intellectuals scattered throughout the world?

"I've located Costantino," I said. But had I mentioned Costantino to the Professor? And how much had I told him? I asked myself if I had said too much . . . if that were the reason for his not making a solid proposal.

"Really?" He no longer seemed interested in hearing the details of my life.

To go back to Italy would have been a triumph. Over arrogance. Over condescension. Over all the things I had fled from.

I thought I wouldn't have the Machine to keep me company any longer. I thought Costantino had called me only once, in the late afternoon, to say, "I don't want to pressure you."

I don't remember the few comments the Professor and I exchanged that evening. I don't even remember if the oysters and quiche were good or not. The rhubarb sorbet was unusual and very good. I promised myself I would try to make it.

At ten o'clock I took a couple of pills and went to bed.

Monday: Gateau des Adieux

I

The only parts of the Machine I had left on were the alarm, the coffee maker, and the toaster oven. So I didn't tape my dream and when I woke up I didn't remember it. I spread some blackberry jam on my croissant. It was quarter to seven, but Professor Cerignola had assured me that he too woke up very early. I phoned him at the Pierre.

"I was thinking," I said, "I'd really like to invite you here this evening. Cancel our dinner reservation. I'll expect you at seven."

I didn't play my usual hand of bridge. Before going to class I polished the silver, rinsed the Capodimonte dinner service and the Murano glasses I keep for special occasions. I put a pad on the table, took out the tablecloth my mother had embroidered, spread it over the pad, and ironed out the folds. I called Mrs. Califano and the liquor store and ordered what I needed. In the subway I jotted down the menu: Cajun jumbalaya, *artichokes alla giudia, gateau des adieux.*

The shrimp I would buy downtown at the Chinese fish market where I always shop. For the artichokes I'd have to stop at Dean & De Luca, the only store in New York that has artichokes comparable to the Italian ones.

I got to my office very early and rushed so that I could get home an hour earlier. I figured it would take me fifty minutes to cook, ten to set the table, and half an hour to put on makeup and get dressed.

When I got home I immediately put a bottle of Collio white and a Franciacorta Brut into the freezer. I began to prepare the shrimp for the jumbalaya. While it was simmering in a terrine, I trimmed the artichokes and started on the cake. It was a recipe from Corsica, as I learned from a not very reliable cooking program on TV. Good, though. Apricots, walnuts, and *crème fraiche*. They used to make it in Bastia—so the chef du jour said—as part of the customary farewell dinner for relatives who were emigrating.

When everything was ready and the table set, I took a shower and put on a pair of black velvet slacks and a red silk blouse. The professor would arrive in two hours.

Jerry was listening to the last lines of one of his favorite movies. "I'm sorry to disturb you," I said.

"Come on in." We knew each other well enough for him to realize that I would not drop in during his sacred hours without a good reason. "Just as an opener," I said, "Kevin

Shell is Costantino. My Costantino from when I was young. I've spoken to you of him."

Jerry aimed the remote control at the TV and turned it off. "That's a really incredible coincidence." He was slurring his words slightly. There was a bit more than a glassful missing from the bottle of Scotch.

"Not exactly a coincidence." I told him the whole story about Mrs. Schelucci, of the tenement, of my move to Turtle Bay Tower. "He knew where I was right from the beginning. It's just that I didn't know anything about him. Not a coincidence. Everything was planned, in a certain sense. Perhaps . . ."

I was about to say that Costantino was expecting to be found sooner or later. That he counted on it. Instead I said, "The extraordinary thing is that he's just the same. The same as I remember him. The puppy had brought in his bowl and so I let him eat with us and then he fell asleep . . ."

I was recounting the episode so badly that the sensation I felt very powerfully then was escaping me now. I tried to be more direct: "Costantino is happy if another creature is happy, and then he's eager to communicate his happiness to you. He was like that at thirteen. He's good. It's a word we don't use much anymore, but I don't know how else to put it."

"Fantastic. And . . . What comes next? What's going to happen now that your good boy has let himself be found?"

I also told him about Professor Cerignola.

"In short," I concluded, "it seems they want me to

return to Italy. So let's say I could have two good reasons for returning."

"What would you do there?"

"I don't know. I like to be coherent and honest about the things I agree to do, but I feel I've lost touch with my thoughts . . . Suppose you've grown up in a certain way because you're right-handed and then you learn your life might have been shaped differently because in fact you were left-handed. At that point does it make any sense to sacrifice yourself in the name of a principle that may not even apply to you? And above all, if the principle of tolerance my father taught me is right, then wouldn't it be absurd to fixate on any decision whatever?"

"Don't ask me," he answered. "I don't believe in tolerance. I believe in conviction."

"I know. You're in good company. Everybody believes in conviction. Everybody's super-convinced about everything. At times it seems I am the only one capable of contemplating one idea, no matter how brilliant, and suddenly—at the same moment—being struck by a completely opposite one. It must be my left-handed idea. It lurks there in the dark. It's there with all its reasons behind it, because there are reasons, for everything. I never feel protected by my own opinion nor by my belonging to the group that shares it. I seem to be the only one who doubts and believes that perpetual doubt is the only opinion that's morally decent and rationally tenable."

I got up from the sofa and took a few steps toward the darker side of the room. Without turning toward him, I added, "And if that weren't enough, the dog has also destroyed my work on the Machine."

Jerry had never understood the meaning of the task I had set myself to. I had discussed it with him only superficially, then I hadn't spoken to him further about it.

"I'm sorry to hear that," he said.

"Well . . . It was all an illusion. Two years thrown away. A naive project. To reach people's hearts, to create a marvelous detour in the course of history by means of a machine for warming croissants."

I went back to the sofa and sat down next to Jerry. "And now don't tell me you knew it all along."

"No, I won't. Talk to me about Costantino. Would you leave him just when you've found him again?"

"It's not that simple. Don't think it's a single choice—one package containing both Professor Cerignola and Costantino. It's a dual choice: to go or not to go to Italy with the professor—that's if he asks me to—and to decide to attempt the impossible with Costantino. Here or in Italy, it doesn't matter. We're both grown-ups, we have enough free time, seven hours' flying time is nothing. Oh, that's if he, too, asks me."

"He hasn't?"

"In a certain sense, maybe. But I'm not sure. I haven't given him much time."

"And so?"

"And so I have to make up my mind whether to let myself be tempted into accepting a position I'm not convinced about, on the one hand, and on the other to really want to start something up again that was perfect, that was never spoiled. The position I'm not persuaded about could be a marvelous revelation."

"And the perfect love of your adolescence?"

"That could be a catastrophe. Two difficult choices."

"Nonsense. Every time our path comes to a fork, the two directions we're confronted with are always simple alternatives. Ambition is very simple. Love is very simple. The spirit of adventure is very simple. Revenge is very simple. And fear, and laziness, and egotism are also very simple. And finally there's death, the simplest thing of all."

He was advising me—if I understood him correctly—to be courageous, he of all people, who kept himself shut up in his apartment, surrounded by shadows that emerged at night from his old movies and old books. It seemed to me he had never made a choice, that when he arrived at the fork he stepped back. Or maybe not? His way of life so indifferent to the model the new mythology presented to us every day of how life should be lived, couldn't it itself be a product of free and courageous choices?

He was sitting next to me—a thinner Cary Grant, with beautiful blue eyes behind his glasses. He put his hand on mine.

"You're an angel," I said.

He skipped to a very different subject. "How long has it been since you've made love with a man you know well? Someone who matters to you?"

I took my hand away. "What do you mean?"

"Don't get angry. Think about it. How long has it been since you've had a steady lover, how long has it been since you've had your morning coffee with a man instead of with a machine?"

I couldn't help thinking that at least I had got married eons ago.

"What about you?" I asked. "I don't think you have such a great love life."

"But I don't want one. I'm not made for it, and I have the good sense not to get involved in situations I'm not cut out for. You're a woman who should have a husband . . . children . . ."

"You're just like my sister. Not even my mother was so old-fashioned as to talk to me like this."

"You're keeping love outside your life and sex at the edge of it. Like something smelly you keep on the window sill."

"You, too, it seems to me. You've never introduced me to any of your girlfriends. Who are they? Who's ever seen them? You don't go out with them too often, as far as I can tell."

I was talking to him rather mechanically. My thoughts were elsewhere. Everything changed when I began to fear

AIDS, I kept telling myself. I hastened to have all the tests and swore that never, with anyone, would I have but ultra-safe sex. Jerry took my hand again and began to kiss my palm. And at that point—I kept telling myself—that's all there was to it.

"At that point, that's all there was to it," I said aloud.

"What?"

"Once I'd decided that no partner—not even the closest and steadiest—could be trusted . . . AIDS, you understand. Even an apparently nonpromiscuous man could have a faithful wife who had a brief encounter with an ex-fiancé, who in turn had had a brief affair . . . The most elementary precaution is to treat anyone as if he were a stranger. So it might as well be a real stranger."

Gideon was the manager of a moving company. He wrote acrostics lauding peace among men, love of nature, respect for the wild. But I didn't know that when I picked his company out of the Yellow Pages to move my furniture from my old apartment to Turtle Bay Tower. I called him to arrange the move and he asked for my phone number. I gave him the Romance Language Department's number. "You must be a teacher?" he asked. He was thrilled. He faxed me his acrostics.

When the movers loaded the furniture, he came along with them and helped unload and arrange it in the new place. He stayed behind when they left. We made the bed together with the new sheets that had just arrived from Macy's. We got into the shower together and scrubbed each other. He was very blond and very big, a veritable tower. He carried me to bed in his arms as if I weighed just a few pounds.

Later, as I sat alone in front of a dish of penne with mint, it struck me I could have invited him to supper. I was watching *An Affair To Remember* on TV. Then I turned off the light and fell asleep trying to remember the details of our encounter. He was big and thick and blond. OK. He wrote acrostics, but I certainly didn't remember where I put his faxes. Then what? He told me he liked intellectual women. "They're much sexier than the others." He phoned me once or twice, but I always told him I was busy.

The full moon, flat and chalky, was suspended over Queens in the sky that was still light.

"And so," asked Jerry "what happens at that point?"

"So much for that is what happens. So much for being a stranger. He doesn't disappoint you, he isn't demanding, he doesn't become a habit."

"This millennium is ending badly," Jerry said.

"We're in it, too. You and I. What are you doing to prevent the millennium from ending badly?"

"I try to find a few moments of happiness. I try to place my respect and my disrespect where they belong. I drink a few Scotches. I don't mix with people I don't like. I read. I listen to music. I watch movies that show me an innocent world." He slipped his hand under my blouse and began caressing my breast. "You're very dear to me."

"I know. You're dear to me, too."

I let him go on. I had the feeling he was trying to comfort me. After a while I kicked off my loafers and pulled down my slacks. The sun was setting on the other side of the city and was painting the facades of the buildings in Queens red. A triangular flock of Canada geese flew by heading south. While Jerry undressed, I pulled my blouse over my head and threw it aside. Jerry took me in his arms and carried me to bed.

Afterward he got dressed and then, tenderly, dressed me, gathering my clothes that lay scattered across the living room. He ran his hand through my hair, caressing and arranging it at the same time. It seemed rather than make love to me he really wanted to show me something I couldn't understand on my own.

I remembered what he had said a little earlier. It's true, I said to myself, this millennium is ending badly. There are only solutions to small problems. According to him, I just broke the ice. Is that the idea? I had finally made love with a man I knew and admired, whom I found attractive, whom I loved. OK, I said to myself. It can be done. We got out of bed, I for sure and he, too, I think, with a slight and not unpleasant feeling of nostalgia.

We knew that first time was also the last. Nothing had

been spoiled. We were closer friends than before. We reheated some leftover coffee and shared it, then I went back to my apartment to wait for the professor. As I inserted the key in the lock, I turned toward Jerry, who was standing in his doorway. "Everything's going to be all right," he said.

2

The professor arrived exactly on time with a small bouquet of gardenias.

"You're very attractive," he said. "A true Italian beauty."

He came right to the point as he sipped the Franciacorta I had served him as an aperitif. "We're offering you a job as a cultural consultant to the Chief. Speeches, press relations, TV appearances, publicity. There'll be experts in every field, from politics to the media, and you'll have to coordinate them in a certain sense, you know, the cultural, intellectual image. You'll have to work it so that our rivals can attack but not ridicule us . . ."

He shot a number at me that was six times greater than what I earned at the university.

"It's a lot," I said.

"It would be a big job . . . And you wouldn't be alone. I've contacted personally a number of other Italian intellectuals who've not yet found a position worthy of them. You would make a formidable team."

I went to the kitchen and turned on the deep fryer. I laid the artichokes in the wire basket.

The professor followed me and stood leaning against the doorway while he sipped his brut.

"You would be given all the means to complete your work."

I didn't want to think about the Machine anymore. But how could I not imagine myself in Italy? In Italy. At Costantino's side. Well paid, honored, respected. My hands were trembling. Watch out, I said to myself. Don't get burned right now. I reheated the jumbalaya and brought it to the table.

"Dinner is served," I said. And I added, "The fact is I have a different orientation." I pointed out the photograph of Giacomo Matteotti, the socialist leader killed by the Fascist in 1925. The picture, in a gilded frame, had belonged to my father. It hung over my desk along with other ones: my sister with her children; Mother and Father on their wedding day; Giuseppe Verdi, dressed in black, walking in the main piazza of Busseto; Dino Campana; Giacomo Leopardi; Henry James as a young man in the painting by La Farge, and myself on the day of my graduation, between Doctor Paoletti and Signor Ceccarelli. "It seems a bit pretentious when I say it like that, but, as I told you, my heart's on the left side."

"But dear girl, do you really think there can be in Italy—or anywhere else in the world for that matter—the slightest possibility of political choice in making government policy? Don't you see that whoever holds public office has only one road ahead of him? Our party is trying to put people in charge who are trained for the job, who aren't going to steal and who don't belong to the gang that has ruled the country till now. That's all."

I went to the kitchen to lower the basket of artichokes into the boiling oil. I set the timer at five minutes to turn off the fryer and raise the basket. I went back to the table and served the casserole.

"The fact is I'm afraid of you," I said.

"You're afraid of us? You mean you're afraid, if those are the terms we're using, you're afraid of the right?" He tasted the jumbalaya, and then added: "You're a fantastic cook." He went on: "Think of our country. Let's take one of its problems as a case in point. We don't have tramps falling drunk in the streets, but we do have other . . . individuals who for many different reasons represent a small or big loss for the national economy. Let's suppose that responsible Italians, the ones who produce, suddenly decide not to carry the losers. What do you think would happen?"

I didn't answer and let him continue. He put his hand on mine and gave it a couple of paternal taps. "What would happen is that a good many of these . . . individuals would wake up, get some initiative, and in a short while would become assets in our society."

"And the others?"

"The others would drop out of the race. They'd fall by the wayside, they'd give in, thereby providing an even more radical solution to their problems. It's sad, my dear, but true."

I took my hand out from under his and reached for a piece of raisin bread. I buttered it and then left it on my plate. He had hesitated twice before saying 'individuals.' I wondered if he'd been tempted to use some other word rather than such a bland one.

"It is true, dear professor, but it is sad," I answered.

"It amounts to the same thing."

"Not at all. It's like a bottle that's half full for the optimist and half empty for the pessimist. They're two very different things. You're saying that it's so true that we shouldn't worry if it's sad. And I say it's so sad that I don't care if it's true. So you see, it's exactly the opposite, forget 'the same thing.' That's it. Perhaps it's the only real and irresolvable difference remaining between the right and the left. *It's sad but true*, or *It's true but sad* . . . You can cheat a little—on one side as well as on the other—by denying either one or the other terms of the antithesis. By naming the objectives and hiding the costs. But you can't deny the antithesis. I face it from one direction, you from another."

I reached for the piece of buttered raisin bread, and put it down again. Instead, I ventured to give the Professor a couple of affectionate taps on the hand. "You don't deny that it's sad, and I don't deny it's true. But there's an enormous parallax—as my father would have said—in the thing as you see it and as I see it. Because our points of view aren't different, they're opposed, as you know perfectly well."

"Pardon me, but I don't believe that. I can't believe that a reasonable and liberated woman like you could be taken in by irresponsible sentimentality."

He fixed his deep-set, intense eyes on me. He seems like a Neapolitan actor, I said to myself, and suddenly I recalled a role Vittorio De Sica played several times and unforgettably: the tricky lawyer, his toga draped with studied carelessness, his argumentation paradoxically flawless.

"My dear, you don't truly believe that the politics of pragmatic choice are merciless. You can't but perceive what deep, irresponsible, childish, narcissistic mercilessness lurks beneath ideological hypocrisy."

I leaned under the table and offered the buttered piece of raisin bread to the puppy. The professor continued speaking.

"Do you really think that bringing our country to ruin, knowing full well it will be our children who will pay for our gut humanitarian impulses, is acting responsibly and justly? Does an intelligent woman like you truly fear the right?"

After he finished his raisin bread, the puppy went into the bathroom and came out with his bowl in his mouth and brought it to the table. I shelled a shrimp and fed it to him with some rice.

"I certainly do fear the right." I cocked an ear to the sound of the frying artichokes. The casserole was perfect.

"And you're not afraid of the left?"

"No, I am on the left."

"I'm speaking of communism. You said you were democratic. Would you like to live the way they lived in Prague ten years ago?"

"Absolutely not. But that's a closed chapter. Forever, I think." I went to get the artichokes.

Professor Cerignola relished the shrimp dish and was praising the artichokes. "Only Piperno's in the Roman Ghetto can prepare them like this," he complimented.

"And besides," I went on, "I'd hate to leave New York. I've learned to like life in this city . . . I've found the best and most honest wine store in Manhattan just three blocks from here, I know where I can go in Queens to buy top appliances at discount prices. I know all the bus and subway lines. I know the movie houses where you can see the latest films for three dollars. I know how to avoid the cashiers with long painted fingernails who make you wait endlessly in line because of their clumsiness. I can find theater and opera tickets at half price. I've adapted and I'm happy."

He increased the offer, but I told him that wasn't the point.

"I see," he said. "And so?"

I got up to get the cake. It was beautiful, the top perfectly browned, light and raised. I put dessert plates on the table and sat down again.

"And so?" repeated the Professor.

"And so I have no choice but to be what I am. And I'm beginning to understand who I am. Also thanks to you and to the fine dinners you've given me and the attention you've paid me. I assure you I'm infinitely grateful. It's much easier to express a thought when we know it's not falling on deaf ears."

"So you won't hear of returning to Italy and helping us do our task?"

Before I could answer, he had his last mouthful of cake, put his fork down on the plate and laid his hand on mine. "Because you know we're doing our best, don't you?"

"I'm sure you are. But I can't do that sort of best. Last night the dog erased all the dreams from the Machine. Now there's nothing left. Only a tape that goes on for eight hours, blank as the conscience of a newborn child. This little animal in his wisdom has shown me what I was laboring to deny. Dreams do not accumulate, unfortunately, and therefore do not form a reality. No Machine can prove the contrary. Although we can't formulate this truth satisfactorily, we have no choice but to accept it. All the alternative identities—the ones in the dreams and the others that never had the opportunity to come into being, my left-handed self included—might have been, but they're not. They have been on the verge of existence, but they didn't make it over the verge. The one who made it is sitting here in front of you, in black trousers and red blouse. I haven't even turned the Machine back on. I never will. Except for croissants and coffee. It's been quite a disappointment, believe me. Years of work to come to the conclusion that there aren't any answers in the Machine. And the proof of that was given me by a two-month-old puppy."

We went to sit in the armchairs. The dog followed us and fell asleep curled on my feet.

"There aren't any answers in the Machine?"

"No, not in the Machine, not in playing bridge by myself, not in the hypothesis of a left-handed I. I've gone back to the point I was at two years ago: to the simple decision that an aggressive, intolerant attitude will not do for me. Why not? Because simply not. The proof that that's right, proof capable of touching if not the intelligence, at least the heart, that proof I haven't found. The Machine serves no purpose."

"I'm sorry."

I brushed it aside with a wave of my hand, as if it weren't important. But it was, very much so.

"What does accumulate is life, day after day. It accumulates and forms a solid reality. I am what I am because I've lived whatever's happened to me, be it written or not written in my destiny. I am who am. Jehovah says so in Genesis. Jonathan Swift muttered it in his genial madness as he lay dying. We all pause sooner or later to consider it. I am what I am and I have to behave on the basis of that. It's my responsibility. The choice I made coming over from Italy was the right one."

"I think so, too. But probably now the right one would be to come back. Things have changed, believe me."

"Not for me. There wasn't room for me in your rivals' camp, at that time . . . Now maybe, but it's too late. How could I forget the frustration of those days . . . when criticizing minor things like press censorship, the gulags, the self-confessions gave your schoolmates the right to call you a fascist, for instance? I'm not that noble. I would forget everything if I were really afraid of you, but I am not."

The Professor beamed. "Now you're talking," he said. "Come with us and you'll see that nobody will stop you from being anti-Fascist and proclaiming it."

"I'm sorry. I really don't belong with you."

He was silent for a moment. Then he said, "You are an extraordinary cook." He was a dear man. I enjoyed watching him eat my meal.

The doorman called on the intercom to let us know Professor Cerignola's limousine was waiting.

"I'm sorry I wasted so much of your time," I ventured. "I should have told you right off there wasn't any chance. Only I didn't know. The dog had to teach me."

He waved my apology aside. "It wasn't a waste of time. I'm honored to have met you."

At the door I gave him a kiss. "Good luck," I said to him.

"To you, too. From the heart."

He walked down the hall, short and slim in his impeccable, pinstripe, right-wing suit. I doubted he would go on feeling comfortable as a member of his team. For the time being he was driven around in a silver limo, but I wondered how long this would last. Before turning the corner to the elevator, he looked back and smiled at me.

3

It was ten-thirty. I didn't want to call Costantino, but the telephone sat there temptingly. I took off my clothes and put on a pair of casual slacks and sneakers.

People were still in the streets. I hurried over to Sutton Place and sat on one of the benches in the little park along the river. I pulled up my collar and stuck my hands in my pockets. Is there, I thought, a way of breaking open the Ego's petrified shell and for one sublime moment become something else—a person, an animal, a plant, a cloud? It would be the most intoxicating and at the same time the most instructive of adulteries. The bliss of being free for a moment from the deadly trap of being constantly oneself. To break through one's armor and let oneself occasionally be seduced by a different opinion, by a preference one doesn't share.

For all this I had tried to find the formula, a key I could hand to the world, so that this millennium might die redeemed from the original sin of intolerance and the next might have a clean start. The Machine and I, shut in a room away from the world and witnesses and objections. Crazy idea. What tricks did my mind contrive to eliminate all opposition to its purpose?

The little park was a cocoon of impenetrable darkness

and quiet. The lights in Queens were rings and yellow stripes painted on a distant black backdrop. Their rays couldn't reach me from across that space, and even the city's traffic noises did not penetrate the silence that enveloped me. I thought if this whole tale should really turn into a lesson for you, it would be the shortest I ever taught.

I was hoping the Machine would let me find the words to articulate what I felt, but it didn't work. There are no answers in the Machine. An absolute solution to the ancient vice of the Absolute cannot be found. The millennium will end badly, as Jerry predicts, and I can't do anything about it. Someone else will have to.

I had hoped to find the words. "*Nisi enim nomen scieris cognitio rerum perit*," says St. Isidore. If you don't know the name for them, the notion of things is lost. I haven't found the words for you, nor for myself. And, believe me, without possession of the word, keeping a grip on things becomes a hard task.

But wait a minute. I'm the one who runs on the treadmill for an hour at top speed, who makes her bed every morning tight and square as a cardboard box; I'm the daughter of a man who wound his Movado Kalendomatic even as he lay dying, and of a woman who filled the pantry every year with bottled jams, marinated eggplant, tomatoes, artichokes in oil, pickled peppers arranged neatly on paper-lined shelves, the stickers on the bottles from the previous year washed off in warm water and replaced by fresh ones labeled in violet Pelikan ink with an old-fashioned fountain pen.

And I have a sister who's succeeded in becoming a northerner, complete with blond hair and blue eyes, and who has produced two children who look like Germans. Even that, I suppose, takes self-discipline, although it's a strange discipline of forgetting, while mine is the opposite, a discipline of remembering.

I will keep a grip on my thoughts, even if I didn't succeed in linking them to the right words, in labeling what I had in mind in violet Pelikan ink so that anyone could reach for the jar and make use of it.

A sign read: "No dogs." I realized it was cold out. When I got on a bus to go back home it was almost midnight.

I won't call my children Dexter, Saville, or Kenneth. I won't leave a homeless man to die alone on a sidewalk. Nothing will convince me that capital punishment is necessary. I won't ever believe a bidet is an unbecoming fixture. I'll go on loving this country and I'll go on being in part an outsider.

There, my tale has ended. I haven't found the words. I haven't found the means of convincing you, because, you see, it isn't up to me. I've only recounted a story to you. Lorenzo da Ponte and Mozart told a love story about a maid and a butler, and, in parallel, a story about a count and a countess as secondary characters. It's just a story. Marat, Robespierre, and

Danton made the French Revolution. But *Le Nozze di Figaro* still works. And the French Revolution? A lot of heads cut off and after a few years Napoleon is portrayed wearing a crown and ermine robes. And so? Forget it, I've lost the train of thought myself.

I've told you a story; I can't do more than that. The plot opens at the point in which the adolescent Martina, still one and apparently indivisible person, is lying on the moss on Poggio di Mezzo next to her Costantino, or on or under him, wrapped around each other. And from there unravels the thirty-year-long double spiral: the solitary bridge game with the foursome multiplication, the Machine, with the multiplication by the 365 dreams of every year, then the left-handed twin with the simplest and most significant multiplication of all, by two.

All right. Now the story's happy ending should be the plot tying up its loose ends on a lightly sketched drawing—otherwise what purpose would it have served? Something that tells who I am, but doesn't lock me into what I am: into the fatal trap of intolerance, the Iron Maiden of Nuremberg that pierces your heart and brain as she closes shut. To finish the drawing, a pencil should accent only the humbler points—the laundry in the basement, a dish of well-prepared pasta, love for a dog. There is nothing alarming here. Here the two halves can stop spying on each other.

But they shouldn't be reunited, though—heaven forbid.

We want the two halves, standing in for the four bridge hands, for 365 days' worth of dreams and many other possibilities. And both there, in their valuable duplicity, to represent the Proximus of whom I spoke in one of our most boring class sessions, and to protect him from intolerance if one of the two halves should assume an advantage over the other, let pride go to its head and begin to think it's something special, ever unique, forever.

But without spying on each other. Side by side in harmonious coexistence. That way they could be somewhat at peace, but please, not too much so. Not the sepulchral peace of Absolute Truth, of unlimited self-importance, of unshakeable opinions. Stand by me, my left-handed twin, and laugh at me if I begin to take myself too seriously.

So here the story has ended. After all it's very simple. Everything that's linked in my memory is real; everything that's real entails obligations; respect for the obligations of others doesn't exempt me from fulfilling my own. Spontaneity is the only condition that enables me to live fully, but with the accumulation of memories it's only natural that I've become less natural. I can resist this ineluctable process to a certain extent, but I might as well resign myself to accepting most of it because nothing further can be done.

It's absurd claiming to recover a condition of innocence. It's more than absurd, it's dishonest. It's like postponing one's actions until an impossible condition is met.

The bus lulls me soothingly. I'm looking at an ad that says IT'S EASY. It's in the form of a triptych: a fat girl on the left side, in the middle an exercise machine called Slim-Step, and on the right the same girl weighing forty pounds less. It's easy, it's easy. Losing forty pounds, saying I love you to a man, making a decision, not believing in absolute Right, and knowing what's right for me. Luckily, I don't have to lose forty pounds. The rest of it I'm convinced I can do. It's easy.

What I really want to make clear is that I didn't take the Slim-Step ad as a message from God. I presume that if God decided to get in touch with me He would choose a less trivial medium. I took the assertion literally, as I always do. A reasonable assertion, though not of divine origin. If you are determined, it's easy to lose forty pounds. With or without, I might add, the help of Slim Step. What's difficult is to have the determination.

I feel at peace, even knowing that it won't be easy for us two, for Costantino and for me. The problem is how to succeed at being unnatural with sufficient *naturalezza*. I can only express my meaning in Italian, because the word "naturalness" that I found in the dictionary a few days ago has for me such an unnatural ring. Does "naturalness" really translate "*naturalezza*," a word that means a way of being, of behaving, of living, of feeling, without always being aware of one's being, behaving, living or feeling? A way of letting oneself plunge into life, accepting it rather than confronting it? I wonder.

And even in Italian, although I'm familiar with the word, I long ago lost what it refers to, and so has Costantino. And so has my country, so decrepit, cunning, tricky. And so has this country, which isn't young anymore either.

But this country—this city rather—is mine, too, by now. It's true I don't understand it, but I know it. I've learned its essential etiquette. In the West Village it's a sign of friendliness to smile at people one passes on the sidewalk, while uptown it's considered indiscreet and intrusive to make eye contact with a fellow rider during a forty-floor elevator trip. And in every part of the city you can pet dogs, but never children, or you'll be taken for a child molester.

As I enter the lobby through the revolving door, Mr. O'Mara smiles benignly at me. I race through the rain forest and manage to get into the elevator just as the door is sliding shut. Two KLM stewardesses, milk-and-honey blondes, six feet tall with athletic shoulders, have already pressed the penthouse button for the health club at the top of the building.

The elevator takes off with a whoosh and stops at my floor. I step out on to the sage-green carpet in the hallway and smile at the Valkyries, who continue on their way to further, incomparable fitness.

As I take my key out of my pocket, the pale blue of my apartment door seems to dissolve and take on a mirrorlike surface that reflects an image of me in green corduroy jeans, checked shirt, tweed jacket, holding a key in my hand.

I pause for a moment. The mirror image I see, which is what I am only in reverse, will open the door and walk through the narrow foyer and be welcomed by a jubilant puppy madly wagging his tail and fat little bottom simultaneously, his ears laid back like two pink rose petals on each side of his round face.

And I know this time I'll bend down to pick him up, slip my hand under his soft belly, take him on the bed with me, and let him lick my face. I'll let him remind me with his incomparable *naturalezza* and immense capacity for love of the *naturalezza* I left behind, where Costantino left his as well, among the heather of Poggio di Mezzo.

And I'll tell myself if it's not possible to return to Italy by accepting Professor Cerignola's offer, it may be more likely that I could by marrying Costantino and finding a way of life that truly fits me as I am—as I was born and as I've become, by destiny and by error. I could publish a book every two or three years and bid farewell to teaching. Or the easiest thing, which is staying in this country, renewing my green card and achieving something here, as so many have done these last three hundred years.

And if it's hard to forget Italy, no one, fortunately, will compel me to. And if it's hard to love a man, it's certainly easy to love a dog, so why not begin with this foundling fate has sent me? Then I'll try loving Costantino again, and making him love me; on this or that side of the Atlantic, or a little here and a little there. After all, what's seven hours' flight time?

And one sure thing, God willing: this will be my last left-handed dream, the last time I'll be wondering whether I am on this or that side of the mirror, whether I'm petting my dog with my right or left hand. And to this little trusting creature I'll say with complete *naturalezza*, come, boy, I'm going to call you Bonzo. And I will have this dog, this life, and everything else, including Costantino and my two countries.

And now that that's decided, I turn the key, open the door, smell the basil on my window sill, and I'm home.

Martina's Tête-à-Tête Cookbook

I

RISOTTO ALLA MILANESE

1 big beef ossobucco (the marrow is used for the risotto; the meat and bone are used for the broth)

2 cups Arborio rice

2 ounces butter

1 Spanish onion

1 glass Pinot Grigio or another dry white wine

a pinch of good quality saffron

grated Parmigiano Reggiano cheese

(a nonstick pot will be useful)

For the Gremolata: the yellow rind of half a lemon, Italian parsley.

For the broth:
the bone and meat of the ossobucco

1 carrot
1 onion
1 stalk celery
1 ripe tomato
salt and pepper
8 cups water

After assembling all the ingredients for the broth, boil for one hour.

Chop onion and simmer with the bone marrow and half of the butter. When golden brown, add the rice and stir constantly for two to three minutes. Add wine and cook until the wine evaporates. At this point, you may leave the whole thing alone and resume the cooking when your guest has arrived.

Add two cups of hot broth, lower the heat and let cook for about 20 minutes, stirring occasionally and adding more broth if necessary. Taste for salt. When almost ready, add the saffron.

For the Gremolata, chop very finely the lemon rind and the parsley. The Milanese usually add the Gremolata to the ossobuchi that they eat with the risotto, but it is very good on the risotto itself. So add the Gremolta when the risotto is ready and you turn off the heat. The risotto itself should not be too liquid or too solid. Creamy is the right texture. The last step is adding the remaining butter. Let the risotto stand for two minutes and serve with Parmigiano Reggiano.

2

LOBSTER ARMORICAINE

1 medium-sized fresh lobster

1 scallion, chopped

1 onion, chopped

2 ripe tomatoes, peeled and cubed

2 good pinches of chopped Italian parsley

horse radish

4 tablespoons extra virgin olive oil

1 glass dry white wine

the juice of one lemon

1 cup fish broth

2 tablespoons cognac

1 pinch of cayenne pepper

1 clove chopped garlic

2 ounces butter cut in small pieces

Cut the lobster tail in even pieces along the natural connections. Cut the shield lengthwise, discarding all stony substances contained in the pocket. Set aside the intestines and coral. Put the cut pieces of lobster in a pan with three tablespoons preheated olive oil. Sear quickly and then remove the lobster. Now wilt the chopped onion and chopped scallion in the oil, stirring constantly. When the ingredients turn pale gold, add the chopped garlic clove and the tomato cubes.

Arrange the lobster pieces over it, add the wine, the cognac, and the broth. Cover and cook in hot oven for 15 minutes, then extract the meat from the lobster pieces and arrange on a serving tray. At the same time place the pan on a very high flame in order to reduce the liquid. Add the intestines and coral to the liquid, stirring constantly. Turn off the heat and add the butter, whisking until creamy smooth. Add cayenne pepper and lemon juice, pour the sauce over the lobster and garnish with parsley.

3

SALMON EN PAPIER

2 thick salmon fillets
2 zucchini
2 carrots
1 celery root
1 Spanish onion, sliced
salt and pepper
extra virgin olive oil
oven paper
dill
mint

Julienne all the vegetables (except for the onion, which should be sliced separately) and dress them with oil, salt, and pepper. In the middle of two separate oven-paper sheets place the julienned carrots, zucchini, and celery root. Place the salmon on top of them and the onion slices on top of the salmon. Wrap the paper to form two bags.

Place in hot oven for about 25 minutes or until the paper starts to brown. Then open the bags and broil for a minute or two until the onions turn brown. Sprinkle with chopped dill and mint, then serve.

4

CARCIOFI ALLA GUIDIA

4 artichokes

4 cups cold water

the juice of one lemon

salt

4 cups of peanut oil (The artichokes should swim in the oil. Don't worry, they will not absorb it if you proceed correctly.)

Put the water in a mixing bowl and squeeze in the juice of the lemon.

To prepare the artichokes, remove the coarse leaves, cut the tips of the tender ones, cut the stem until you have two inches remaining, and then peel the stem. Soak the artichokes in lemon water until ready to fry. Dry them on a cloth, then open the leaves and press them down to form a rose.

Slightly preheat the oil and then start frying the artichokes on a low fire. As soon as they are moderately golden, fish them out, put them on a paper towel, and let them cool for a minute while you turn up the heat under the frying pan. Put the artichokes back in the very hot oil and sprinkle with salt. Fry until they turn dark gold and then dry them well on a paper towel.

5

ASPARAGUS SOUFFLE

1 bunch of asparagus
2 eggs separated
2 cups milk
2 tablespoons flour
2 tablespoons butter
salt and pepper
grated Parmigiano Reggiano

Cut the tips of the asparagus and set them aside. Cut away the bottom of the stalks until only the green part is left. Put remaining stalks in the milk and heat until boiling. Then process milk and stalks in a blender or food processor until smooth. Add the asparagus tips to the mixture after you stop processing it. Melt the butter in a skillet over low heat. Add the flour. Then slowly add the asparagus mixture and cook for a few minutes. Let it cool for a little while and then add the Parmigiano Reggiano and egg yolks. Beat the whites stiff and then fold them in. Pour the mixture in either a porcelain or a glass pan—something that is presentable because a souf-flé is served in its cooking container. There also should be enough room in the pan for the rising that will occur while the soufflé is cooking. Preheat the oven to 370 degrees and bake for 20 minutes. Do not open the oven during this period. Then reduce the heat to 300 and continue baking until the soufflé is slightly brown.

6

RHUBARB SHERBET

$^{1}/_{2}$ pound young rhubarb stalks
10 ounces of water
1 cup sugar

Peel rhubarb and cut into small pieces. Boil in water for 30 minutes, covered, over low heat. Check occasionally and add water if necessary to avoid complete evaporation. Add the sugar and process in either a food processor or blender until smooth. Pour into an ice cream maker and follow the manufacturers instructions. Otherwise set in a deep freezer for 1 hour, stirring two or three times during the freezing process. Serve with whipped cream.

7

PORCINI AND POTATOES SAUTÉ

2 large Idaho potatoes

1 pound of fresh wild mushrooms, preferably porcini

10 leaves of calamint (If you can't find calamint, use half fresh mint and half fresh majoram.)

extra virgin olive oil

salt

Cube the potatoes, put them in a pan with olive oil, and toss them with your hands. Put them to cook on a midsize burner and turn up the flame. Clean the mushrooms and line them up on a towel. Stir the potatoes until they begin to brown, turn the flame down to low, and cover. Move the pan of simmering potatoes over to a small burner and set the flame to low. Cut and cook the mushrooms in a wide frying pan over the largest burner with the flame set on high. Scatter 10 leaves of calamint on the mushrooms. Empty the mushrooms into the pan with the potatoes, raise the heat, stir it for a minute, and then serve.

8

GATEAU DES ADIEUX

10 ripe apricots, pitted and cut in wedges

10 walnuts, broken in half

8 tablespoons unsalted butter

8 tablespoons crême fraiche

$1^1/_2$ cups sugar

2 eggs

1 cup all-purpose flour

$^1/_2$ teaspoon salt

$^1/_2$ teaspoon baking soda

$^1/_2$ teaspoon baking powder

Melt 3 tablespoons butter in a 9" round, nonstick baking pan that is at least two inches deep. Coat the sides well and leave the remaining butter on the bottom. Sprinkle evenly with $^1/_2$ cup sugar. Nicely arrange walnuts and apricot wedges on the sugar layer.

Beat eggs with 2 tablespoons crême fraiche.

In large bowl, mix flour with remaining sugar, baking powder, baking soda, and salt. Add remaining butter (softened) and remaining crême fraiche. Blend until batter is stiff, then add egg mixture little by little, always scraping sides of the bowl. Pour the batter over the apricots and bake in preheated oven at 350 degrees for about 35 minutes until a knife inserted comes out clean. Invert on a serving platter after 5 minutes. Serve cool with whipped cream.

8

GATEAU DES ADIEUX

10 ripe apricots, pitted and cut in wedges

10 walnuts, broken in half

8 tablespoons unsalted butter

8 tablespoons crême fraiche

1$\frac{1}{2}$ cups sugar

2 eggs

1 cup all-purpose flour

$\frac{1}{2}$ teaspoon salt

$\frac{1}{2}$ teaspoon baking soda

$\frac{1}{2}$ teaspoon baking powder

Melt 3 tablespoons butter in a 9" round, nonstick baking pan that is at least two inches deep. Coat the sides well and leave the remaining butter on the bottom. Sprinkle evenly with $\frac{1}{2}$ cup sugar. Nicely arrange walnuts and apricot wedges on the sugar layer.

Beat eggs with 2 tablespoons crême fraiche.

In large bowl, mix flour with remaining sugar, baking powder, baking soda, and salt. Add remaining butter (softened) and remaining crème fraiche. Blend until batter is stiff, then add egg mixture little by little, always scraping sides of the bowl. Pour the batter over the apricots and bake in preheated oven at 350 degrees for about 35 minutes until a knife inserted comes out clean. Invert on a serving platter after 5 minutes. Serve cool with whipped cream.